"A month! You expect me to stay here for a month!"

A stab of apprehension ran through Vida. Her voice shook. "Karim, you have no right to keep me here. You've made it abundantly clear you despise me. What satisfaction can you possibly get from tormenting me like this?"

"The satisfaction you denied me on our wedding night, of course," Karim replied calmly. "Here in Morocco you are most certainly still my wife and before I'm prepared to end that relationship, you'll not need to be reminded of that fact."

"No! You're mad!" Vida responded in disbelief.

"You may be right," Karim said quietly. "Perhaps it is madness to think that possessing your body will do anything to heal the pain knowing you has caused me."

ANGELA WELLS left the bustling world of media marketing and advertising to marry and start a family in a suburb of London. Writing started out as a hobby, and she uses backgrounds she knows well from her many travels for her books. Her ambitions, she says, in addition to writing many more romances, are to visit Australia, pilot a light aircraft and own a word processing machine.

Books by Angela Wells

HARLEQUIN ROMANCE
2790—SWEET POISON

Moroccan Madness

Angela Wells

Harlequin Books

TORONTO • NEW YORK • LONDON
AMSTERDAM • PARIS • SYDNEY • HAMBURG
STOCKHOLM • ATHENS • TOKYO • MILAN

Original hardcover edition published in 1986
by Mills & Boon Limited

ISBN 0-373-02844-X

Harlequin Romance first edition June 1987

CHAPTER ONE

THE cold June rain stung Vida's face as she stepped outside the lounge bar of the Black Swan. Having felt obliged to accept Amanda's invitation to celebrate the other girl's forthcoming wedding after the office closed for the day, she had contented herself with toasting the bride-to-be before slipping away as soon as possible, leaving the little crowd to enjoy themselves without her.

The taste of champagne still sweet in her mouth, she bent her flaxen head against the scurry of wind that sent the long silken tendrils flying.

Her presence wouldn't be missed, she admitted sadly, aware that the girls regarded her reserve as stand-offishness—perhaps even vanity, and the men resented her lack of personal interest in them as a sign of frigidity, which insulted their images of themselves as virile attractive males.

Frigid! Her mouth twisted wryly. If only they knew how wrong they were! Once she had wanted nothing more than to give herself to the man she loved with total commitment and an almost slavish desire to please. What was it Karim had said he expected from her? She suffered a pang of nostalgia as she recalled the beauty of his intense face, the passionate mouth and the dark compelling eyes that had magnetised her with their power as he had told her, 'I want nothing more than any man requires from the woman of his choice . . . that she should serve and respect me, keep herself beautiful for me . . . and bear me sons.'

5

She had recognised the softly spoken conditions as being deliberately provocative to tease her, but at the same time there had been an element of truth in them. For all his European veneer, Karim's instincts had borne the deep grain of his Middle Eastern origin.

Damn her wayward thoughts! The last person she wanted to think of was Karim Gavigny. That episode in her life with all its passion and its trauma was behind her, irrevocably ended. She was as distanced from Karim emotionally as she was physically. The night she had escaped from Morocco had ended that episode of her life with the finality of a funeral.

Vida found herself standing at the bus stop, her feet guided subconsciously as her conscious mind refused to relinquish its post-mortem of the past.

Karim Gavigny. It was inevitable his image should persist tonight of all nights, she supposed wearily, staring at the rain-spattered glass of the framed timetable on the post in front of her. She had been working in Tangier at the time. April it had been, she remembered, a North African April just over a year ago. The nights had been cold, but the days had been filled with sunshine. How she had loved it. The colour, the parade of different races, the sheer cosmopolitan atmosphere of the city had enthralled her. In its exotic warmth and colour she had begun to bloom.

It had been touch and go whether she had accepted the offer to go to the company's North African branch to work with Greg Dolman as a translator. Consolidated Minerals was an expanding company and their interest in the North African minerals and mining industries something of a new venture. Greg himself had been a shrewd operator, a superb mineralogist and executive, but his knowledge of French had been hardly better than schoolboy basic. Vida had a gift for languages. It was something she accepted without conceit. Just as some people had perfect pitch so she had an ear for language, not only its accents, but the nuances of idioms.

When Consolidated Minerals had advertised for a bilingual secretary she had been given the job over twenty other applicants. Still she had thought deeply about whether to take the three months overseas tour when it had been offered to her. Although she had been twenty-two she had been shy and reserved, lacking the self-confidence she had felt necessary to tear up her roots, spindly though they were, and launch herself into an alien environment.

It had been Greg himself who had persuaded her. Already established in Morocco, he had returned to London to select a translator with the necessary technical background. They had clicked immediately, and within days Vida was on her way to Tangier to work on the new extensive programme Consolidated Minerals were launching in French-speaking Morocco.

Greg had done everything to make life easy for her, even to the extent of arranging for her to live in the same block of flats as himself and his wife, and he had introduced her to the social circle in which they circulated. She had been to their dances and parties and had felt some of her natural reserve diminishing.

She had had an escort to these events, Tim Haydon-Smith, blond, six feet tall, a couple of years older than herself. She had found him a pleasant, light-weight young man. Public school and university-educated, he had been a product of the old Empire. His forebears had owned rubber plantations in Malaya and more recently tobacco farms in Zimbabwe. His parents had made their fortune and got out when times turned bad, but Tim had never been brought up to work. He had learned how to spend money but not how to earn it. His ambition had been to marry a rich woman. He had had the looks and breeding to do it, and until he met the female who fitted his plans he had been quite happy to escort Vida to the social occasions where she might be found.

A shudder traversed Vida's body as memories she had tried vainly to erase rose to the surface, bubbling into her consciousness with the insidiousness of a poison gas.

A year ago something had turned this pleasant, non-consequential young man into a monster. She didn't know then what it was, and she didn't know now. Over the passing months she had tried to put the images of his outrage from her mind, but it had been impossible.

In the long lonely nights after she had fled back to England the events of that evening had tortured her memory.

She was shivering now, standing at the deserted bus stop, her eyes probing into the storm-induced murkiness for a sign of the transport which would take her back to her flatlet.

Karim. Try as she might, his image persisted in her mind's eye. She might never have met him if it hadn't been for Greg and his niece Sara.

Sara Dolman had erupted into her life two weeks after she had settled in. Greg had been apologetic because at sixteen Sara had been a will-o'-the-wisp, a free-and-easy traveller who never thought of danger or disaster, imagining everyone was as honest as she herself was. Red-haired, curvaceous with a joie-de-vivre that was intoxicating and contagious, she had brought a new dimension into Vida's newly expanding life.

'I'd appreciate it deeply if you could keep an eye on her,' Greg had confided the day afer Sara's arrival. 'My brother's let her come here believing I can control her.' He had shrugged his shoulders. 'But to be realistic, there's not a lot I can do, and I have a feeling with all the temptations around she could get herself into quite a lot of trouble, unless someone curbs her enthusiasm!'

Vida had been sympathetic, knowing Greg's wife lived in a world of her own that was still full of English tea and cucumber sandwiches with Brahms recitals in the evening. Sara was a different generation, a free spirit confident of her own power of survival. Vida's added years had told her Sara's sophistication had never been put to such a stringent test as it might face in Tangier—the crossroads of the world where two ancient continents touched. She had agreed willingly to befriend the teenager.

'A disco!' Sara had said beseechingly to Greg, having dropped in late one afternoon just as they were about to leave the office. 'I've met this super young man and he wants to take me to a disco tonight! Surely you can't object to that?'

'Well, I can't approve if I've never met him!' Greg had been querulous, responsibility for the young, nubile teenager weighing heavily on him.

'Vida knows him,' Sara had asserted truthfully, adding with not quite so much veracity, 'and she likes him!'

'I've certainly met Khalil,' Vida said carefully. 'And from what I see he seems a very pleasant young man. As a matter of fact Sara and I were on the beach when we got tar on our feet and it was Khalil who came to our rescue. He showed us how to get rid of it by using orange peel.'

'So he's a greengrocer!' Greg had been quite belligerent. 'That hardly proves he's fit to take my niece out for the night.'

'Honestly, Uncle!' Sara had expostulated, her cheeks pink with anger. 'You're not being fair. Khalil is on holiday from Rabat University. His family is of French origin and he's staying with his brother in Tangier for the next couple of months. I can't see what possible objection you have to our going out together!'

'Only that this isn't England and some of the tourists who come here every year have given the impression to the local youth that women from Northern Europe are extremely free with their favours. It's a situation that's proved embarrassing at the least and disastrous at the most for some young women who still respect themselves!'

Greg's homily might have been old-fashioned, but it had brought Sara to a standstill. Obviously she wasn't as liberated as she liked to pretend, and Greg's warning was not about to go unheeded.

There had been a long silence while Sara digested what she had been told, and Vida pondered on whether to intercede. In her own mind she had been reasonably sure Khalil Gavigny would treat Sara with respect. He was cultured and polite, a composite of French and Moroccan with a charm as attractive as his intelligent boyish face.

'Suppose Vida comes with us?'

'Oh, no! . . .' Vida turned down the suggestion even as Greg considered it.

'That would make a difference,' he conceded.

'You will, won't you, Vida?' Sara had seized her arm, her fingers moving in agitation on its tender flesh. 'Oh, please say you will!'

She should have refused. In retrospect it was the most stupid thing she had ever agreed to. It had revolutionised her life. But at the time, with Sara's pleading face turned to her own, she hadn't the heart to turn down her suggestion. So what if it did mean playing gooseberry? She had moved her shoulders in lethargic acceptance of the idea. 'All right, if it will make you happy.'

A few hours later she hadn't been feeling so tolerant. 'You've done what?' she asked in disbelief, her blue eyes flashing fire across the table of one of the waterfront bars where the rendezvous with Khalil had been arranged.

'Calm down, do, Vida!' Sara made an abortive attempt to placate her. 'Don't be cross, it's just that I thought you might be bored without a partner, so I asked Khalil to bring his friend Raschid with him.'

'Thank you very much!' Even now, months later, Vida remembered how irritated she had felt. Far better to have sat alone in the disco rather than be forced into the company of a strange young man she had seen only once and who could have wanted her company as little as she wanted his. With due respect to his youth and innocence—although the latter might be in some doubt—the teenage Raschid was not the companion she would have chosen for the night, and it had been presumptuous of Sara to have arranged it.

If it hadn't been for loyalty to Greg, the fact she'd given her word and a very real concern for her young friend, Vida would have left then and there. To have done so would have spared her unimaginable grief. But in those days she had been soft. Experience had given her the streak of aggression that now tinted her personality.

'All right,' she had conceded wearily. 'But you pull another trick on me like that and I'll see you carried off to an Arab slave market without lifting a finger!'

'Lovely!' Sara dimpled back at her. 'Do they still have them?' Before Vida had been able to reply Sara had jumped excitedly to her feet. 'Look—Khalil's coming now!' She had paused, her face falling. 'But it looks as if Raschid can't make it. He's alone.'

Ten minutes later, when Vida was beginning to relax in the hope that Raschid had no intention of putting in an appearance, Khalil, looking past her shoulder, stiffened, half rising in his seat. 'What on earth . . .'

She had turned, wondering what had caused him to exclaim. Everything seemed normal. Certainly there was no one in sight vaguely resembling the young man she had met briefly on the beach.

It was Sara who, astutely following Khalil's gaze, had clutched Vida's arm, letting out a low whistle, saying, 'Wow!'

Following her path of vision, Vida saw a man walking purposefully towards them, weaving his way between the crowded tables. Even among so many people so variously dressed, he had stood out.

Now, as if she were watching a video film, Vida relived the scene. Tall and well-built, dressed in elegant slim-fitting grey trousers beneath a body-hugging casual shirt, his dark good looks were dramatic enough to be termed handsome. Probably in his early thirties, he moved with the attitude of a man used to wielding authority—a distance eating, graceful stride that attracted attention. Vida had been impressed. Today, over a year later, she recalled her reaction. He had been a stranger and yet against all the odds he had stirred a dormant recognition deep within her. Her body had tensed and shivered like a dog sensing danger.

'Who is it? Do you know him?' It had been Sara who asked the question.

'I should do.' Khalil had looked confounded. 'It's my brother Karim—but I can't think what he wants here.'

That had been Vida's first meeting with Karim Gavigny. Later she was to learn that he had bribed the adolescent Raschid to stay at home so he could replace him. That Khalil's brother had been aware of her presence in Tangier, had seen her in the street, had watched her, wanted her and had taken the first opportunity of meeting her. Apologising for Raschid's unavoidable absence, he had smoothly altered the arrangements for the evening, insisting they became his guests at the Purple Phoenix, a famous and expensive night club on the outskirts of the town. Only Vida had demurred, suspicious that he should have acted as Raschid's messenger and irritated by his high-handedness. The entertainment he suggested would not come cheaply and she was wary in case there would be a price expected of them in return.

She had been outvoted. Constrained by her responsibility towards Sara, she had had no option but to accompany them. But she had made one last protest, standing proudly to face Khalil's autocratic brother with a simple dignity.

'We're not dressed for a club like the Phoenix,' she had insisted.

It had been an excuse for Karim to look at her, and even now her cheeks coloured as she recalled the intensity of that appraisal. From the light golden tan of her soft skin as it glowed in the vee neck of her dress, down past her breasts to her slender waist, following the flowing line of her simple blue cotton dress to where it swirled round her legs just beneath her knees, his eyes missed nothing. Still his gaze had travelled downward past the long elegant curve of her leg to the fine-boned ankle and slim foot poised in the strappy sandal.

'My dear Vida,' he had said at last, the expression in his eyes unfathomable and a little frightening, 'you are quite beautiful just as you are. You may not be wearing silk or diamonds, but no other woman in the place will outshine your natural loveliness.'

She had found the words flamboyant and disquieting and made a move to protest, but he had added in a low voice, too soft to be overheard, 'Don't argue with me. Do you imagine I would be seen with you if I were ashamed of your appearance?'

She had been stunned by his arrogance, her mouth falling open as words failed her. Undisturbed by her angry glare, he had left her standing there, saying equably, 'My car's parked round the corner. I'm afraid it's a bit cramped for four, but it's only a short ride to my flat.'

He had pre-empted her protest at their destination, his smile gleaming whitely against the light tan of his attractive face. 'You may be perfect—but my brother and I must wear evening dress if we are to be admitted.'

Vida had watched him stride off as Khalil had shaken his head in puzzlement.

'It just doesn't make sense,' he had said.

'He's not generally so generous?' Vida asked acidly.

'Oh, he's generous enough, but then he can afford to be. It's just that . . .' The warm colour had risen in Khalil's face. His embarrassment had intrigued her.

'Just what?' she had prompted with interest.

'That he's always so scathing about the way the women tourists allow themselves to be picked up.' His dark intelligent eyes registered the flash of anger on her face as he amended quickly, 'Some of them, that is. But Karim has always said that if a woman is so easily to be picked up, then it's not worth a man's while to bend down and oblige her!'

'Charming!' Sara had interposed with raised eyebrows. 'Well, he's done a little bending himself tonight, hasn't he?' She nudged Vida conspiratorially. 'See if you can't burn his fingers before he drops you again.'

It had been a suggestion that appealed to Vida. If she had any idea how to put Khalil's sardonic brother in his place she would have had the greatest joy in so doing. In the event it was she herself who had been scorched before their final parting.

It had been difficult not to be impressed by Karim's car when he returned that evening. Vida had let her eyes rove over the sleek golden body of the Maserati Khamsin, hoping to display only a casual interest, as if she drove around in such an expensive vehicle every day.

But Sara had no such qualms.

'Fantastic!' she had breathed, running her fingers lightly over its streamlined bodywork before adding wistfully, 'I don't suppose you ever let anyone else drive it.'

'That's quite right, I don't.' Even now Vida could hear the beautifully modulated tone of his voice with just a hint of amusement colouring it. 'A beautiful car is like a woman. It responds best to the touch of one master.'

The arrival of her bus took Vida by surprise. So deeply engrossed in the past had she been, she only became aware of it as its bulk slid to a stop beside her.

Gratefully she climbed aboard, paying the correct fare and making her way to the top deck for the twenty-minute ride home.

That evening at the Purple Phoenix had been superb. Whatever had happened since couldn't detract from the pleasure of that night.

She remembered how she had stared at the selection of dishes on the unpriced menu, ranging from a humble grapefruit juice through specialised Moroccan cuisine to such delights as venison and lobster. She had finally selected smoked salmon followed by lamb cutlets provençal. It had hardly been an adventurous choice, but she guessed the price wouldn't be the highest on the menu, although she admitted from what she had seen of Karim Gavigny that he wasn't likely to flinch from the sight of the bill, however high.

It was over the meal that she first began to understand more about her escort. It had started quite simply when he had ordered wine and she had asked him shyly if he was a Moslem.

He had lifted his glass slowly, looking speculatively at her over the rim. 'You think I may be one of those renegade followers of the Prophet who pays lip service to Islam but drinks wine with the infidels in their houses of shame?'

Vida had blushed scarlet at the mockery in his tone, furious that he had the power to make her feel gauche.

'I'm sorry,' she had apologised stiffly. 'It's none of my business.'

'But I'm flattered by your interest,' he had protested. 'No, I'm not a Moslem, nor could I claim to be a Christian. You see before you a man without religion or even a culture with which he can truly identify himself.' Relentlessly his eyes had bored into hers.

'My father was born in one of the Trucial States of the Middle East, my mother is Moroccan, but I was brought up from early childhood by my stepfather in Paris.'

'Culture?' Vida had repeated thoughtfully, her mind spanning the differences existing between countries, let alone continents.

Karim had nodded. 'All men are prisoners of their culture,' he had told her. 'They believe what they are taught to believe. They fight their battles, dream their dreams, live out their lives within the standards they are given by their elders.'

'Yet you don't identify yourself completely with the European culture you were brought up with?' she guessed.

'I dislike its air of total superiority,' he admitted simply. 'Islam was a great power when Europe was full of savages. The Arabs gave the world mathematics, exquisite architecture, music and poetry. The troubadours who carried the message of courtly love to the uncivilised courts of Europe came from Araby.'

His expression had been challenging, and she had been unable to escape the feeling she had been undergoing some kind of test.

Quietly she had risen to the challenge. 'I, too, respect Islam and its customs.' As if it had been only yesterday she recalled her reply. 'But, as you say, man is a prisoner of his culture. Although I may respect the customs, my own upbringing makes it unlikely I would ever embrace them, while you . . .'

Karim's eyes had narrowed, assessing her closely as she had plunged on, 'While you, surely, have the unique opportunity of standing apart from both cultures and finding out for yourself what you really believe in . . . what you really feel?'

'And with that opportunity, the danger of discovering I believe in nothing . . . and feel nothing!'

Vida had been mesmerised by the pain in that admission and flattered by his confidence, then he had smiled, a slow charismatic smile that had made her heart plummet alarmingly as the tension left his face. But it had happened then, at that time. Her heart had reached out to him. Her own life had not been so happy that she couldn't recognise the evidence of a deep-seated sadness. Although she wasn't aware of it at the time, afterwards she was to know with absolute certainty it was at that moment she had begun to fall in love with Karim Gavigny.

Later that night before they parted he had kissed her. Khalil and Sara had already left the car when he had held her back with a light hand on her arm.

'I think we could let them walk through the park to your apartment and take their time to say good night to each other, don't you—*petite chaperone*?' Dark eyes wicked with amusement had mocked her.

'I'm not a prude,' she had defended herself stiffly.

For an answer Karim had put out his hand, placing it gently beneath her chin, tilting her face slightly upwards to gaze at her steadfastly. She had felt herself tremble, suddenly desperately aware of his latent masculinity strong and vital behind the patina of wealth and respectability. She had felt her heartbeat quicken as she had stared back at him, conscious of the tension simmering between them.

To her dying day she would remember what he had said. 'There was a lily and a rose in her face. There was sunset in her hair, and dawn smiled upon her lips . . .'

Later she discovered it had been a quotation from the Persian poet Gilbran. At the time she had been flattered and moved by the way he had delivered the compliment, letting her gaze drop in confusion from his eloquent eyes to rest on his mouth. Strong yet tender, it mesmerised her. She could imagine those hard silky lips against her own.

His face had come closer. His hand moved from her chin and his mouth brushed her lips, teasing and taunting until she succumbed to his loving assault. She had welcomed the intrusion of his tongue: excitement like an electric current passing down her spine, tantalising her, tormenting her. She forgot she had never kissed or been kissed with such exquisite sensuality in her life. She forgot she had only known the man who was pleasuring her mouth so intimately for less than eight hours. She forgot his opinion of easily available tourists and that with the unrestrained offering of her warm soft mouth to his sweet adventuring tongue, symbolically she was offering him much, much more!

The bus shuddered to a halt as Vida regained her senses. She had to stop torturing herself with memories like this. Karim and everything he had once meant to her were in the past never to be recalled. Resolutely she stared out of the window, taking a perverse pleasure in seeing the cold rain slanting down, so different from the hot skies of Morocco where she would never set foot again.

Bending her head against the lashing rain as she alighted from the bus, Vida started on her five-minute walk to the flatlet where she lived alone. Luck had been on her side there at least! Arriving back in England with enough money to last her a couple of weeks, she had spent the first anguished night in a small hotel.

It was the receptionist who had taken pity on her pale face and dark-circled eyes and who, without too

much probing, had elicited that she was homeless and
desperate and had put her in touch with a housing
trust run by a charity. Their function was to buy up old
houses and turn them into self-contained flatlets for
'single working gentlewomen'. It was an archaic
description, but there had been nothing old-fashioned
about the way the charity functioned or the accommo-
dation they provided.

Vida had been accepted as a suitable tenant without
formality, and once more fortune had smiled on her
when she had been re-employed by Consolidated
Minerals.

Standing in the porch, she pushed the strands of
sodden hair away from her face, reaching inside her
raincoat pocket for her key.

It was the slight creaking of the gate that warned
her she wasn't alone as a man came towards her, dark
head down against the buffeting of the wind.

Something about him reminded her of . . . but no,
she was being absurd. Her mind had been too locked
in the past to relinquish its memories; besides the face
was thinner than she remembered, the likeness surely
only a passing one?

The key slipped from her nerveless fingers as her
throat throbbed dryly. She was having illusions,
perhaps hallucinating the whole figure? Stooping, she
searched on the wet ground for the key, but a man's
hand beat her to it. She saw it held between slim
fingers, heard his voice, attractively accented, say
hesitantly, 'Vida?'

It was no illusion. White-faced, she faced him,
instinctively squaring her shoulders. Whatever he
wanted he couldn't hurt her. She was here, in her own
country, and she knew something that he didn't . . .

'Khalil?' There was still a question in her voice,

although she had ceased to doubt his identity. But he had changed. In one year Khalil Gavigny had turned from a fresh-faced, carefree twenty-year-old to a hollow-cheeked man. As his head dipped in acknowledgement of her recognition she asked tremulously, 'What—what brings you here?'

'You,' was the succinct reply. There was no glimmer of a smile on his face, no acknowledgement of the fun they had once shared during Sara's short stay in Tangier. Nothing but a harsh regard that turned her blood to water, as his measured tones continued hardily, 'Karim wants to see you again. Your husband has sent me to take you back to Tangier!'

CHAPTER TWO

'I'M afraid you've had a wasted journey.' Her voice sharp to the point of rudeness, Vida was still unable to abandon the absurd idea that her thoughts had somehow conjured up the young Moroccan out of the thin air with the mystique used by the illusionists in the Medina, who could make solid objects come and go like phantasmagoria.

Yet her eyes told her Khalil was flesh and blood; the substance of his youthful body making its impression on the comfortable armchair she had waved him into after allowing him access to her home.

Perhaps the coincidence wasn't remarkable. After all, wasn't today the first anniversary of her doomed marriage to his brother? Wasn't that the reason Amanda's pre-wedding party had conjured up the past so vividly? Why shouldn't it be the same reason that had spurred Karim into this incredible action?

Vida stood uneasily, her hand resting on the back of the other armchair, trying desperately to summon her senses together.

Khalil was staring at her almost as if she were a stranger instead of the girl he had laughed and joked with before her deepening relationship with his brother had thrown a barrier of circumspection between them. Was his reticence because he still thought the worst of her or simply because he still saw her as his brother's wife and as such sacrosanct?

Of course she knew he had always held Karim in awe. Being half-brothers probably had as much to do with that as the sizeable gap in their ages. Karim had been born of a race unknown to his younger brother. He himself might remember nothing of his father or his country, but he had inherited the former's pride and passion, his courage and determination. Karim might have lived with his mother's second husband in Paris since he was three, but he had been born of a desert people renowned for their stoicism and bravery, and their qualities had been bred into his bones. This, at least, Vida had learned about the man she had married in the heady days of their brief courtship.

She stiffened involuntarily beneath the loaded valuation of Khalil's sombre gaze, resenting the feeling of guilt it engendered in her. 'Well?' she asked sharply.

'I've been told to let you know my brother has decided the time has come to end your marriage officially. He wishes to see you again so that a settlement can be made on you to terminate the contract with honour.'

Her pulse quickened alarmingly. 'I want nothing from Karim. To be honest, when I didn't hear from him I assumed he'd already divorced me. After all,' she added with unconcealed distaste, 'it's easy enough for a man to get a divorce in Morocco—especially in the circumstances . . . or rather in what your brother assumed the circumstances to be!'

Khalil lowered his eyes before her icy regard, managing to look awkward and embarrassed. But then he had never had Karim's confidence or self-assurance.

Making a small gesture of appeasement with one hand, he appealed diffidently, 'Please understand, Vida, I'm not totally in Karim's confidence, but I know for a fact he's made no move to get your marriage dissolved until now.'

Vida shrugged her shoulders, her blue eyes cool and reserved, as she concealed the churning emotions within her. Although Khalil didn't know—and she was not inclined to tell him at that time—Karim's actions held no interest for her one way or another. Not since the traumatic day she had finally made up her mind to seek advice on her legal status in the event of Karim continuing to ignore her existence.

She had emerged shaken from the advice centre she had visited, scarcely able to believe what she'd been told—that a woman whose permanent home was in England could not legally marry at all in a country governed by Islamic law, where all such marriages were potentially polygamous.

At the time of her marriage in Morocco she had still been officially resident in England, working for a British company, subject to U.K. tax laws ... and Karim by Islamic law could already have had another wife, or have been contemplating taking another one. Under the present law in her own country it seemed she had contracted a 'potentially polygamous' marriage—which made it automatically void.

She should have been delighted; instead she had experienced a feeling of utter devastation. To have gone through the ritual of dissolution would at least have given her brief love affair some standing. To deny the very existence of their contract was to relegate it to nothing: to obliterate the passion as well as the pain.

She had barely listened as the consultant had gone on to tell her that there was a strong feeling within pressure groups that the existing law was discriminatory and there were already moves afoot to have it amended. In the meantime, she was counselled, she should apply to the courts to have the record set straight . . .

It was a step she had never taken. What was the point? If she wasn't married, she wasn't married. The knowledge alone was enough. She needed no court documentation to specify her shame!

Her face a mask of uninterest, she betrayed nothing of the inner turmoil her memories had evoked.

'Karim must do as he wishes. It's no longer of importance to me—after all, he cares nothing for me, and frankly I find his offer insulting. I'm not prepared to be humiliated just because your brother wants to play out the role of a humanitarian Moorish lord!' she snapped, angrily moving round the chair to fling herself down on it, outrage visible in every aspect of her attitude. 'That's the message you can take back to Morocco with you!' she ended fiercely.

How dared Karim ignore her existence for so long and then choose the anniversary of their wedding to twist the knife of his scorn in her heart! How she had longed to see him again in those early days of separation, hear from his own lips that he knew he had misjudged her. The nightmares of those weeks of useless waiting had left their scars.

Twice she had written to him, begging him to believe her, pleading her innocence, throwing herself on his mercy, his avowed love . . . and she had heard nothing. Now he had the temerity to send his brother as a messenger to take her back to Morocco! A divorce settlement, Khalil had said. Did that mean Karim intended to insult her by publicly disowning her? He must be mad if he thought she would stir as much as an inch to go in his direction!

'Perhaps if you'd consider the idea a little longer?' Khalil's brown eyes pleaded with her. 'It is, after all,

normal procedure in Islam when a marriage breaks
down. The wife is never abandoned without being
fully provided for.'

'Unless she's been discovered committing adultery
in which case she's generally put to death!' Vida
responded tartly, watching with acid amusement as a
blush suffused the young face in front of her. Her
eyebrows winged towards her hairline. 'Do I understand from your last remark that Karim has decided to
embrace Islam as a religion now?'

'No, not exactly, that is . . .' her visitor stumbled
unhappily. 'You know Karim. He has his own code of
ethics.'

'Yes, I know Karim. He's cruel, ruthless and totally
devoid of understanding or compassion!' Vida turned
her head, unwilling for Khalil to see the tears that
scalded her eyes.

'Yet he is concerned about your present welfare,'
she was reminded softly.

That was a laugh! The time to think about her
wellbeing was long since past. She was astounded by
this approach, suspicious of its genuineness, unless . . .
A burgeoning spur of hope kindled inside her.
'Khalil?'

'Yes?' He met her gaze frankly.

'Has anything new happened? I mean, has Karim
discovered the truth behind what occurred that night
at the Villa?'

His eyes swept her eager features with surprise. 'But
he's known that for a long time,' he responded simply.

Vida stared at his composed face, aghast. All these
months of waiting before Karim had deigned to put
her out of her misery. Dear God! Once she had
believed he had loved her as deeply as she had loved
him. Now it seemed he had punished her for the way

she had fled from him by sentencing her to a year of agonising frustration and despair.

'What is the truth' she asked in a voice suddenly hoarse. 'Why did Tim Haydon-Smith force his way back into the Villa when I was alone there on the night of my wedding and threaten to rape me? Why, when we'd never been anything more than casual friends, did he make me strip at knife-point? Why did he half-suffocate me with a pillow so I was practically senseless before thrusting himself on top of me on the bed? Why did he wait there without violating me until Karim burst into the room? Why, Khalil, why? And why did he pretend to my husband that we'd been lovers from the time of our first meeting?'

Her voice rising hysterically, she was only barely conscious of the way Khalil's face had whitened. Making a determined effort to bring herself under control, she clenched her jaw, halting the angry flow of words.

When she was able to speak again with dignity, she asked simply. 'What is the truth?'

Khalil's face was bleak as he drank in her distress. 'I—I didn't know what had happened,' he faltered at last. 'All Karim told me was there had been an argument between you, that he had left to take a matter up with Haydon-Smith and while he was away you went to the airport and took a seat on a charter flight back to England.'

'Well, now you do know.' Vida suppressed her anguish with an effort, adding challengingly, 'Perhaps you, for one, can understand how I felt!'

Karim hadn't understood at all. He had been flaming, furiously mad. He'd become a devil, an avenging demon who hadn't seen her shock and distress. No, her fiery Arab husband had seen only the pale flesh of his possession exposed before another man and he hadn't listened to her pleading sobs, hadn't seen her fear or sensed the trauma she had experienced.

Her breath came in a great gasping sob as painful images sprang to mind. Tim had pushed away from her as the door opened, backing off the bed. She had struggled to sit up, the pain in her throat and mouth almost unendurable. She had been so utterly relieved to see Karim, reaching out towards him in supplication. 'Oh, God—oh, Karim . . .' Her voice had been husky from her ordeal, and he had just stood there looking at her, his face impassive.

Why, oh, why didn't he rush to her and take her in his arms? She had swayed towards him, her blonde hair tangled across her face, tears streaming down her cheeks, hardly aware of her nakedness or the swollen tissue of her mouth where Tim had abused her: too disturbed to feel gratitude that her assailant had stopped short of rape, or even to realise his slim boyish body had shown no evidence of uncontrolled desire. That knowledge had dawned on her many days later.

Karim had taken two steps towards her, and it was then she had seen the hate. She had read in that look that the beautiful, perfect object he had bought as a wife had been handled by another man and had lost its value. Now, when she needed his comfort and protection as she had never needed them before, he had withdrawn them.

As in a dream, she had watched Tim backing away, moving behind Karim as he stood rooted to the spot, burbling something about their having been lovers, having been unable to resist another few hours together: but it was Karim, her husband, who had dominated her attention, as his bleak eyes raked her naked body, his skin the colour of ivory against the blackness of his gaze.

With a sense of total disbelief she saw him ignore her pleading arms and turn away.

She had called out to him in anguish, 'Karim, don't leave me! Oh, please, please don't leave me . . .'

She meant she needed him beside her. She needed the comfort of his arms, his warmth and understanding, but above all she needed his love to wipe out the memory of Tim's horrific action.

Eyes as cold as glaciers had flicked across her, the contempt plain as she drew the pillow in front of her, forcibly reminded of the pitiful picture she made.

'No, sweet wife,' Karim had said with awful deliberation that chilled her like an arctic wind, 'I shan't leave you. I have a matter to settle with your lover first, but be assured, I shall be back.'

Then while she had stared at his proud, cruel face, he had addressed her once more with studied venom. 'You lying little whore!' Karim had said with scathing clarity. 'With all your looks of innocence, your pretence of purity, you really are nothing better than a scheming whore!'

His hand had lifted. Trembling she had cowered away as his accusation stirred an even deeper memory that had burnt its way into her teenage memory with caustic effect. But this time there was no violence, just the deceptively gentle hold of his hand beneath her chin as he turned her face towards him.

'No, I shan't strike you,' he had said with dreadful quietness. 'That's not what whores are for. They're for taking and using: and that's what I shall do with you for the rest of our wedding night. I shall take you and use you, and what you don' t already know, I shall teach you painstakingly and thoroughly, so that when

you crawl out of your bed tomorrow morning there will
not be one *fille de joie* on the waterfront at Casablanca
who will be able to teach you how to better your trade!'

He had gone—striding violently from the room,
leaving only the trembling atmosphere, disturbed by
his icy fury that had turned a deaf ear to reason.

Vida hadn't understood what had happened to her
or why, only that she could bear no more. The revenge
Karim had promised would be too terrible to endure
from the man she had given her heart to. If the
physical abuse didn't injure her, then she would
certainly be left emotionally scarred.

Somehow she had pulled herself together, dressed,
packed the minimum of clothes and phoned for a taxi
to take her to the airport.

By the early hours of the next morning she was in
England.

'I'm sorry, Vida. I—I had no idea . . .'

With an effort she made herself face Khalil, as he
stumbled out an apology. Her face had told him even
more than her words and she could see he was shaken.

'I—I told you, Karim has said very little about what
happened. I just know what I've been told, and what
happened afterwards when he caught up with Haydon-Smith on the road to Rabat.'

'Yes?' Vida found she was holding her breath. Now
at last she would learn the young Englishman's
motivation for ruining her life.

'It was a couple of kilometres up the road when
Karim overtook him and forced him into the side of
the road. He hauled him out of the car and made him
confess the truth. Afterwards there was a fight . . .'

'But what did Tim tell him?' Vida was almost beside
herself with anticipation. She had waited so long to
learn why she had been selected as a victim in such a

bizarre plot. How much longer was Khalil going to keep her on tenterhooks?

'I don't exactly know what he said . . .' Khalil had the grace to look ashamed. 'Only that Karim was satisfied.'

'Oh, no!' Vida wailed in disappointment. All the past months Karim had known the reason for Tim's assault and still he had been unable to forgive her for being a victim. The fact that she had been sullied in his eyes had been enough to prevent Karim from getting in touch with her regardless of what he now knew, but the least he could have done was to let her know he absolved her from blame before this! It was a bit late to discover he had a conscience—and she certainly wasn't going to give him the satisfaction of salving it. He had left her to suffer in ignorance for a year, and she hated him for his wanton cruelty. In all that time he might have had the courtesy to answer one of her letters!

'Please, Vida,' Khalil had seen the distress that contorted her expression and was quick to take advantage of it. 'It means a great deal to Karim that I take you back with me.'

'Does it?' she queried coldly. 'Then he's going to be disappointed.' She met his beseeching gaze defiantly. 'Your brother has treated me appallingly, and much as I like you personally, I resent very much his sending a messenger on his behalf. If his desire to see me again is so strong why didn't he come to England himself?'

Was it her imagination or had Khalil's face gone even paler?

'There's something else I should tell you,' he said tightly.

Now what? Impatiently she wondered if Karim's sudden decision to divorce her was because he wanted

to marry again. She recalled Karim's Uncle Fuad
detailing the charms of his stepdaughter, a nubile girl
called Laila. She had met the teenage Arab girl several
times during her stay in Tangier and had genuinely
admired her glowing, youthful beauty. If Karim
wanted a docile, obedient consort prepared to put up
with his wilful pride, he wouldn't have to look beyond
those soulful, kohl-rimmed eyes!

'Well, what is it?' she demanded with small
tolerance.

Khalil stood up, thrusting his hands into the pockets
of the smart oatmeal-coloured suit he was wearing,
and started to pace up and down the floor. Vida
watched him thoughtfully. He had never been relaxed
since his arrival. Understandably so, in view of the
delicacy of his mission, but now he was as tense as ever
he had been.

She knew something was wrong the moment he
started to speak, avoiding her eyes and jerking the
words out as if they came from some badly rehearsed
script. 'I told you there was a fight. Towards the end of
it your compatriot seized an iron stanchion lying on
the rough edge of the road and struck out at Karim
with it. The second blow struck him across his
back . . .'

A sickening dread riveted Vida's gaze on the
Moroccan's face as the pacing stopped and Khalil
swung round to confront her; a bone-dissolving horror
that turned her legs to jelly. 'Was he badly hurt?' she
whispered. The harshness of his expression made an
awful cold sickness rise inside her. 'For pity's sake tell
me!' she implored, as a blood-chilling premonition
warned her of disaster.

'The bar caught Karim across the lower part of his
back, shattering part of the spine. A piece of bone

pierced the spinal cord . . .' There was an aching silence before he said simply, 'Karim was completely paralysed from the waist downwards.'

Vida tried to fight the nausea as blackesss closed on her. It was as if she was gazing down a tunnel that was growing narrower and narrower. Karim, whose superb body had been a worthy citadel for the proud spirit it housed; Karim, who had gloried in swimming and riding; Karim, whose beautiful male flesh had quickened against her own promising her a breathtaking fulfilment of all her dreams . . . Karim. Karim was paralysed?

A minute ago she had thought there could be no punishment severe enough to make him suffer as she had suffered. But paralysis?

Strong young arms held her, pushed her head gently down on to her lap and gradually the faintness passed.

'Oh! no . . . Oh, no . . .' she moaned softly. Her arms wrapped round her body, she rocked herself, held in a distress that couldn't find the comfort of tears.

No wonder her letters to Karim had gone unanswered in ths personal crisis he had undergone! Perhaps if she'd been there, been able to speak to him . . . But no, she was fooling herself. There would never have been a reconciliation. Karim who, in his thriving business as an antique dealer, handled some of the greatest art treasures the world had known, who loved perfection, hadn't been able to accept the fact that another man had stripped and seen her, imprinted the shape of his body on hers. Karim had never loved her; he had merely loved the way she had looked. He had endowed her with virtues no human woman could ever hope to possess. She was lucky the union had never been consummated. In time she would be able to wipe all thought of her disastrous liaison from her mind.

Surely it was only the frustrating, tantalising ignorance of Tim's motivation in attacking her that dreadful evening which kept the incident alive and sensitive in her imagination? Karim knew the truth. Apart from Tim Haydon-Smith himself, whom she never wished to set eyes on again, it seemed he was the only one who did.

Suppose she did go back to Tangier? What had befallen Karim put a whole new complexion on his peremptory order for her return. She wanted nothing from him, but it might be in her own emotional interests if she saw him once more, talked to him rationally and without rancour, learned the full story before leaving him with dignity.

Wearily she brushed her hair away from her face. Since Karim was prevented from seeking her out, it seemed she had no alternative but to obey his wishes. Only then would she be able to close a chapter of her life that had been short, colourful and as brilliant as the Arabian Nights—a period of Moroccan madness from which her eventual return to sanity had been accompanied by tears and heartache. Only then would she be able to eject his image from her memory as completely as she had managed at last to eject Karim himself from her heart.

'Are you all right?' Khalil's worried question pierced into her consciousnsss.

'Yes.' Vida forced herself to smile reassuringly at his concerned face. 'In the circumstances, it seems I have no option if I want to repeat to Karim's face what I've just told you.' She sighed resignedly. 'I'll arrange to take my summer leave and come back with you.'

Perhaps she should have waited longer before

deciding. She had spoken in the aftermath of shock. Seeing the relief on Khalil's face she guessed how pressurised he had been by loyalty and compassion for his brother.

Even if she changed her mind, there was no way she could disappoint him now she had given her decision.

CHAPTER THREE

IT would be late afternoon before the plane landed in Tangier. Khalil had booked and paid for the flight—in fact he had organised all the travel arrangements so that this act of leaving England had been made as simple as possible for her. How he had matured in such a short time! Not only was there a physical refinement of bone and sinew, but he was no longer the carefree, voluble student she had first known.

Vida was certain the change was more than just the growing-up process. Karim's accident must have been a catalyst in creating the quieter, more reliable young man seated in deep thought at her side.

Even now, a week later, she had been unable to come fully to terms with the catastrophe that had befallen Karim.

She gazed sightlessly from the window. Dear God, how had a man like Karim come to accept being imprisoned in a wheelchair?

The Tri-Star was flying in clear skies over southern Spain. Shortly they would be crossing the Straits of Gibraltar. Within the next few hours Vida would be reunited with the man she had married and deserted. She had learned from Khalil that his brother was living permanently in the large Moorish-style villa he owned in the fashionable part of Tangier known locally as the Mountain, a haven of expensive properties surrounded by ths sweet-smelling pine trees that covered the wooded slopes. He had explained that the flat the two of them had shared in the centre of

36

town had been no more than a *pied-à-terre*, convenient
for Karim's work as a dealèr in antiques and *objets
d'art*: but that after the accident and Karim's release
from hospital the larger residence with its wide
hallways and gracious rooms had needed little
adaptation to turn it into a suitable home for a cripple.

Vida cringed from the word, brushing her hand
across her eyes to take the dampness from her lashes.
It had been in the Villa that Karim had asked her to
marry him.

After their first meeting her initial caution had
gradually begun to melt as Karim had made it clear he
didn't regard her as some cheap and easy pick-up.
Over the weeks of growing closeness he had treated
her with respect, never attempting to force her into
any sign of affection she hadn't been willing to give.
Yet all the time she had been conscious of his desire
for her, carefully controlled, but gaining momentum
as their relationship deepened and matured.

As for her, love had turned her world upside down,
inspiring her to reciprocate the tender kisses he
lavished on her, making her aware of the needs and
longings of her own body as much as those of his. In a
matter of days she had accepted that one day they
would be lovers, that his restrained courting of her was
gathering pace, that her power and desire to keep him
at bay was slowly being undermined, and that when
the time came she would surrender her body to him as
totally as she had already surrendered her heart.

It had been late afternoon when he had taken her to
the Villa for the first time, after a long sun-soaked day
spent on the Atlantic beach. Although it had been
closed, it hadn't been neglected. The polished wood
floors gleamed beneath expensive and colourful
Moroccan rugs, the luxurious curtains at the long

windows glowed with cleanliness. She had been stunned with admiration for the exquisite Capodimonte table lamps, the original oil paintings on the walls and the elegant rosewood furniture. She had found it totally beautiful, and had told him so.

'Would you share it with me, Vida? Would you become my wife and live here with me for the rest of our lives?'

The question had taken her completely by surprise. The enormity of it astounded her. She had stared at him, her blue eyes widening, her throat abnormally dry, wondering if he was joking.

'Don't you know how I feel about you?' he had asked passionately, when she didn't answer. 'All my life I've been waiting for a woman who wasn't only beautiful but who was gentle and honest, who had humour and understanding, serenity as well as passion.' He had taken her unresisting form into his arms, pulling her against the tight, hard curves of his vital body. 'Days before our first meeting I'd seen you walking down the street and known I had to find out more about you. If chance hadn't played into my hands that night when I found out my brother was meeting your friend, I would have still contrived to meet you somehow!' His mouth had traversed her neck from ear to shoulder in a sensual salutation as he whispered his declaration of love against her quivering skin. 'That first night I hadn't been with you for an hour before I knew you were everything I had ever yearned for. It was as if I'd known you all my life or met you again after a parting of a thousand years. I knew our meeting was *Mektoub*—something that is written into the plan of our lives and is inescapable.'

Aching for fulfilment, Vida had clung to him, reaching for his avid flesh with the instinctive warmth

and need of a responsive female. She was being swept
into Karim's dream, but even then she experienced
qualms. Surely she couldn't possess all the qualities he
had listed? A warning voice told her he'd fallen in love
with an ideal and persuaded himself she fitted that
image. Suppose she couldn't live up to his expectations? She had known him so short a time.

'Will you, *mignonne*?' Karim had repeated the
question, his voice throbbing with emotion. 'Oh, my
darling love, say you will!'

Loving him as she did, despite her reservations,
there was only one answer.

'Yes' she had said. 'Oh yes, Karim!'

'I want you so much, want to give you so much . . .'
His hands had moved in urgent caresses, the strong
delicate fingers wreaking their magic through the fine
fabric of her dress. His husky whisper had been
interspersed with soft, seeking kisses placed at
random on her upturned face. 'I want to hang your
neck with rubies and deck your arms with golden
bracelets, adorn your fingers with gems, and then—
and then, *ma belle mignonne*, I want to see you stand
before me wearing all my gifts . . . all my gifts of gold
and nothing else . . .'

She had wanted nothing from him, but to humour
him she had told him happily, 'Yes, if that's what you
want. Then one by one you may remove each of your
gifts . . .' She too could learn to play these verbal
games of love, she thought with satisfaction as she felt
the tremor that shook him.

'Oh, my God, Vida!' Karim had buried his face in
the curve of her neck and shoulder. 'Everything about
you speaks to me of innocence. Even your hands on
my body are uncertain explorers seemingly terrified of
dangers of which they've been told but never known.'

She had felt a blush colouring her face as he detailed her inexpertness, only to feel mollified as she realised what he meant as he continued with the same husky intensity, 'Is it possible I shall be the first man to love you completely? Or do my fantasies become impossible?'

She had smiled then, brimful of desire and affection, and had been thrilled and excited that she could give him the answer he was aching for.

She had wound her arms round his neck, reaching for his mouth with parted lips, breathing her answer into their deepening kiss. 'All your fantasies are possible,' she had told him honestly. 'You will be the first, *mon bien-aimé.*' Then recalling the word he had used, she reinforced her assertion with a sense of deep satisfaction. '*Mektoub*, Karim.'

They had been married a week later in a simple civil ceremony. Afterwards there had been a reception at the Villa, an intimate gathering of friends and Karim's family. Sara had long since returned to England, but Greg and his wife came to wish them well and Vida invited a few of the acquaintances she had made since arriving in North Africa.

Her mother and stepfather had sent their best wishes but had declined to attend, despite Karim's offer of paying all their expenses. Vida had realised sadly but with resignation that her stepfather hadn't approved her decision. But would he have approved of any man she had chosen? she wondered cynically.

It had been early evening with the last of the guests preparing to leave when the message for Karim, from the police, had been phoned through.

He had been furious, but she had realised the importance of the summons. Because of his expertise in the valuation and recognition of works of art,

Karim had been working with the police for some time previously, in respect of a particularly sadistic ring of thieves. It seemed a final link had been made in the evidence, and Karim's expert help was required to identify the authenticity of a thirteenth-century Russian icon. Speed was of the utmost necessity, since any delay could mean the whole ring would be alerted.

Ironically it had been Vida herself who had persuaded him to leave her, for the two hours it would take to make the necessary journey even with the speed the Khamsin could do. 'After all,' she had told him, 'we have the rest of our lives to be together . . .'

She swallowed hard, forcing the sudden surge of tears not to fall. It had been a decision that had shattered her happiness. Shortly before Karim's return Tim Haydon-Smith had returned, forced himself inside the Villa and . . .

No! She wouldn't relive those dreadful scenes again! Her hands tightened round the magazine she'd been reading. How could she have foreseen Karim's terrible accident? But she should have been there. Oh God, she should have had more courage than to run from him like she had. She should have trusted him to get the truth out of Tim and come back to her, if not repentant then at least absolving her from blame.

She closed her eyes, leaning back in her seat. Ashamed of her panic, she sought to justify it with reason. It wasn't only that she had been in a state of emotional shock and physical fear even before Karim had come into the room: it had been the accusing fury of his expression as he had vilified her.

Unknowingly he had used the same terminology her stepfather had used that dreadful night when as a sixteen-year-old schoolgirl she had taken a boy-friend home and been discovered in the sitting room kissing.

'Whore!' her mother's husband had thundered after the boy had been summarily dismissed. 'You cheap, nasty little whore!' He had raised his hand and struck her four times across her face, raising scarlet wheals on the pale skin. She had run sobbing to her room, terrified by his reaction to what had been a gentle adolescent kiss.

But that had been nothing to the horror she had felt later that evening when she had heard her own mother bitterly accusing the man she had married of fancying her own daughter.

'You were jealous!' the older woman had stormed. 'Do you think I'm blind? I've seen the way you look at Vida when you think no one's watching, the excuses you make to touch her. Do you think I don't know you lust after her?'

He had denied it, of course he had. But it had been true. As she lay in the darkness, the pain of the realisation was worse than the soreness of her cheeks where his palm had struck her.

Vida had been four when Lydia, recently widowed by an industrial accident, had married Paul Chalfont. She had grown to love him and treat him as her own flesh and blood without realising the implication of growing into a beautiful young woman who had no blood tie with him. To do him justice Vida truly believed Paul was as shocked by Lydia's accusation as she herself had been, and even more unwilling to give it credence. But the danger existed, and Lydia had sensed it. Both of them knew Paul was no vicious brute to lash out at a woman with either his tongue or his fist. In all her life Vida had never had finger a laid on her before that awful night. Until then he had been patient and understanding, always willing to listen to her problems. Then he had found her exchanging a simple kiss with a young man and all hell had exploded.

Lydia's fervid accusation had shown her the danger she was to the continuance of the marriage of the two people she loved best in the world, and she had known what she had to do. Taking the first opportunity to leave home, she had applied for a linguists' course at a college far enough away from her West Country home to make commuting impossible.

She had continued to exchange Christmas and birthday cards with her family. There had been no admitted gulf between them; she had even stayed with them from time to time. On the surface things were normal. Only Vida knew she had made the change from girl to woman that dreadful night with all the trauma of a premature birth.

When Karim had approached her with uplifted hand and she had cowered away from his fury and condemnation she had known there was only one possible means of escape for her. Once more she had to run.

Startled by a gentle movement across her lap, she opened her eyes to discover Khalil clasping her seat-belt in place.

'I thought you were asleep.' For the first time she sensed a feeling of friendship in his slight smile. 'We're coming in to land,'

Customs formalities were smooth and fast. Vida found she had to tear her eyes away from the departure lounge where she had waited on that ghastly night, half of her praying for the flight to be called, the other half praying Karim would guess where she had gone, would follow her after his confrontation with Tim, beg her forgiveness and take her back with him . . . She

gulped down a wave of emotion: and all the time he
had been lying half dead on the road to Rabat.

'Not long now.' Khalil had seen the strain on her
delicately boned face, felt his own resolution waver
not for the first time since he had gone to London.
Was he doing the right thing in bringing her back to
his brother knowing what he did? But it was too late
for second thoughts now. He masked his feelings of
disquiet, leading her from the terminal building
towards the hired car Karim had sent for them.

Vida sat upright in the comfortable limousine, her
hands tightly clasped in her lap as they sped along the
road to the Mountain. Even in the wake of the day the
air was warm and perfumed, welcoming her back to
the country she had grown to love . . . and the man she
had loved.

As the car drew up before the Villa Vida found her
mouth parched and her legs weak beneath her, glad
when Khalil, glancing at her, sensed her apprehension
and touched her arm briefly in a gesture of comfort.
She preceded him into the large square hall, big
enough for a reception room, remembering the
gracious sweep of the staircase leading to the upstairs
rooms.

'Give me your hand luggage.' Khalil took her cabin
bag, leaving her with only a handbag. 'You know the
cloakroom if you want to freshen up.' He pointed to
the door which she knew led to an elegantly appointed
downstairs shower room. 'I'm not sure which room
Karim has arranged to be made ready for you.'

Glad to wash the travel stains from her face, Vida
carefully replaced her make-up, brushing the shine
from her small straight nose and high rounded
cheekbones and putting some glossy colour on to her
dry lips to moisten their heated surface. Finally she

brushed her shoulder-length flaxen hair to rid it of
tangles, holding it away from her face with a small
velvet band.

Twisting automatically before the full-length mirror, she checked her hemline, but there was no vanity
in the look she spared her appearance. She had chosen
to travel in a simple pale blue cotton suit which
reflected its colour into her eyes, emphasising their
own colour to deep cornflower, but she had grown so
accustomed to seeing her own reflection she perceived
nothing of the startling loveliness that had so appealed
to the dark-eyed admiration of the man who had
determined to make her one of his personal
possessions.

Khalil was waiting for her as she stepped back into
the hall. Silently he led her into the main sitting room
with its opulent couches. The room where Karim had
proposed to her. Vida caught her breath in a torment
of sudden agony. The memory of his impassioned plea
was resurrecting feelings she had thought long since
dead. But he had never really loved her, her heart
wept.

'Karim is coming right away.' Khalil broke into her
thoughts but he avoided her eyes. Suddenly she was
suspicious of the growing nervousness he had shown
since they landed, sensing a reticence in him as if he
had kept something hidden from her.

'What is it?' she asked sharply. 'Is there something
more I should know? Are things worse than you've
told me?' Panic struck her so sharply her voice rose in
agitation. 'Is Karim disfigured as well as confined to a
wheelchair?'

'No.' The voice from the doorway was as deep and
pleasant as she remembered. Spinning round, she saw
Karim manipulate the wheelchair through the open-

ing of the room with the ease of long practice and move across the floor towards her. 'You'll find my face much the same. If time hasn't already blunted your memory.'

There was a quick exchange of glances between the two men, then Khalil slipped out of the room.

Since leaving London Vida had rehearsed time and again what she would do when she saw the man she had married once more. Now she stood speechless, her gaze absorbing his appearance, trying to calm the furious rate of her racing pulse.

He had spoken the truth. There was little change to his face—nothing to bear witness to the suffering he must be enduring. As he had manoeuvred the chair she had detected the movement of the powerful shoulders beneath the thin white cotton sports shirt he wore. His legs, encased in dark brown cords, to her quick appraisal seemed normal. There was no outward sign of his disability, no evidence of muscle wastage or deformity. But then Karim would have ample access to the best medical attention Morocco could provide. Not that anything would compensate, only perhaps alleviate the worst of the effects of the condition.

'And you are even more beautiful than I remembered.' The silky thoughtfulness in his voice was as much a caress as the passage of his eyes as they appraised her from top to toe, sweeping their dark devouring gaze over the curves of her body and bringing it back to rest finally on her face.

'I'm sorry . . . so dreadfully sorry,' she whispered as he continued to watch her with narrowed eyes. 'If only I'd known sooner . . .' She halted miserably, unable to finish the sentence as she found herself beginning to tremble. Please, God, don't let her cry! Karim would be humiliated by her tears, but to see him like this was unbearable . . .

'Yes?' Dark eyebrows rose enquiringly over liquidly brilliant eyes that were even more beautiful than she had dared to remember. 'What would you have done, *mignonne*? Returned to Morocco to taunt me with your beauty, knowing I had no power to extort vengeance?'

'Vengeance?' Vida repeated the word blindly, as a terrible doubt assailed her. Khalil had said Karim had found out the truth behind Tim's assault, but there was nothing in the attitude of the man in front of her to confirm that assertion. Her misgivings deepened as he made an exasperated movement with his hands.

'Spare me the play-acting, Vida. Haydon-Smith confessed the whole plot to me!'

A curious coldness encompassed her. 'What plot?' she asked helplessly, groping her way to a chair and sitting down before her legs collapsed beneath her.

'Fighting to the end to defend your virtue?' Karim's scorn scythed into her. 'Forget it! He told me everything—how you and he had been lovers, how you wanted to set up home together but neither of you had enough money for the life-style you wanted . . .'

'No!' she protested, totally bewildered at what was happening to her. How could someone who had been just a casual acquaintance build up such a dossier of fabrication against her . . . and why?

'How,' Karim continued inexorably, 'when it became obvious to both of you that I wanted you for my wife, you decided between you that you should accept my offer, do everything you could in the following months to disillusion me until I decided to rid myself of you, then taking the divorce settlement you knew was customary in such circumstances, go back to the man you really wanted.'

'You can't believe that!' Her eyes widened with mute appeal.

'Why not?' His mouth hardened. 'What other explanation is there?'

Vida shook her head, feeling as if she were going mad as the nightmare intensified. Tense with growing despair, she blurted out, 'I wrote to you. I told you he attacked me without provocation. He forced me . . .'

'Your misfortune, my beautiful wife, was that you aroused so much passion in your lover that when he overheard that I'd been called away he couldn't resist making love to you just one more time!' Karim cut across her protestation with scathing uninterest. 'Unfortunately for both of you, my business was over sooner than either of you anticipated.' Eyes as dark and hard as coal lingered on her pale face. 'One thing I am convinced of—neither of you meant me to discover you . . . like that. The disillusionment you planned for me would have been of a more subtle nature, ensuring my compassion and thereby gaining you the maximum financial settlement.'

'You're wrong!' Anger was beginning to overtake shock as she met the cold censure he directed at her. 'If you'd ever cared for me in the slightest you would never have believed such lies without listening to what *I* had to say.'

'As I recollect, you didn't stay long enough to say anything very much!'

'Because of the way you threatened me!' Vida choked back the furious scalding tears that demonstrated her frustration. She had had such high hopes of this visit: been really convinced Karim had discovered what had possessed Tim Haydon-Smith to act as he had. Instead Tim's lies had made the situation far, far worse. 'Of course I ran! I was hurt and bewildered, and when you turned on me,' she swallowed hard, hating the necessity of reliving that dreadful moment, 'it was the last straw. It still didn't stop me hoping even up to the time the plane left that you'd have second thoughts, guess where I'd gone and come to me . . .'

'Now you know why I didn't,' he told her calmly. 'Because your lover, not content to take the woman I had just married, also deprived me of the power of movement.'

Despite the turmoil of her own emotions, the sight of Karim's mobile face hardened to the impassivity of an Aztec mask, his splendid athlete's body confined to a wheelchair, wrenched at Vida's heart. Perhaps if she could find Tim Haydon-Smith, with the passage of time she might still resolve the mystery. It was a forlorn hope but one she felt obliged to pursue.

'Do you know where he is now?' she asked in a low voice. The thought of seeing him again sickened her, but if it was going to be the only way then she'd have to take it.

'You mean you don't know?' Karim watched her derisively. 'You just accepted it as a fact of life when he didn't follow you back to England? You accepted that without the dowry I had been set up to provide your attraction for him had waned?'

'I don't have to listen to any more of this!' Vida sprang to her feet, needled beyond endurance by his persistent sarcasm.

'No,' Karim agreed quietly. 'You can always walk away . . . which is more than I can.'

'Oh!' She knew he was deliberately baiting her, but it was clear his pain wasn't assumed. Karim was hurting badly. Perhaps in his own way he *had* loved her. It hadn't been her way, because it had lacked trust.

She held her ground, fighting to regain control of her feelings. Clearly Karim was impossible to reason with. She would try just once more.

'The reason I ask,' she said in a low voice, 'is because it may be possible to force him to tell us the real truth instead of the ridiculous lies you obviously prefer to believe.'

Karim's mouth curled into a cynical smile. 'I think you know as well as I do that that possibility is most unlikely.' But there was no humour in the burning depths of his sloe-eyed gaze as it swept the pale contours of her eager face. 'In fact I don't think you'd have suggested trying to trace him if you hadn't been well aware that he's been dead even longer than I've been confined to this thing.' One hand slapped venomously at the arm of the chair.

Aghast, Vida stared at him. 'Oh, no-o-o . . .!' Her voice broke uncontrollably. Her last chance to exonerate herself gone!

'You really didn't know?' For a second she thought she glimpsed a softening in the adamant face before her, a whisper of compassion in the lustrous eyes, but it was gone so fast it might have been a trick of the fading light. 'He was so anxious to get away from me, he lost control of his car and sent it crashing over the cliffs.' He looked at her shocked face before adding pitilessly, 'I'm afraid your lover burned himself to death.'

CHAPTER FOUR

'I SHOULD have never come back.' Vida felt totally exhausted, her soft words directed to herself rather than the hard-faced man who was regarding her with a brutal disregard for her emotions.

'It's a little late for that realisation,' Karim told her grimly. 'You should have weighed the knowledge of your guilt against the lure of a divorce settlement more carefully.'

'I never wanted a settlement.' She forced herself to make the denial emphatically. 'I came because ... because ...' Oh, what the hell! she berated herself angrily. How could she explain her motives to this contemptuous brute when she hardly understood them herself?

'You came because your avarice outweighed your caution, as I knew it would!' Karim thundered at her, his brows meeting in a straight line on his forehead.

How right she had been to keep her own counsel! This blind insistence on her total lack of integrity was infuriating, whipping her to a peak of self-justification which gave no quarter to Karim's disability. The time had surely come to drop her bombshell in an effort to destroy his pomposity.

'I came,' she stormed at him, 'to tell you to your face that I want nothing from you. I haven't considered myself to be your wife for many months now. Go ahead—get your Moroccan divorce, Karim! As far as I'm concerned I'm already free of you.' She saw the guarded look in his eyes as he absorbed her outburst, and the thought crossed her mind that he had already made enquiries and found out she had never gone through the formalities of getting their marriage annulled. In which case, he was in for a shock, she told herself smugly. 'The fact is, Karim, our so-called marriage was never recognised in England. Because I was still nominally resident there and went through a form of marriage in a country which recognises polygamy, our union was never legal.'

There was no need for her to feel so uneasy as she condensed the facts she had been given, yet somehow she had expected a much stronger reaction from Karim than the steady speculative stare he was subjecting her to.

'I didn't even have to get our mockery of a marriage annulled,' she laboured her point stubbornly so he should have no doubts as to his lack of jurisdiction over her. 'As far as England is concerned, it just didn't happen!' Defiance was in every line of her body and contour of her face, as she concluded crisply, 'I've been living the life of a single woman ever since I returned home!'

'Really?' he drawled, the information seemingly leaving him totally unmoved.

The growing apprehension Vida had felt since his abrasive greeting deepened alarmingly. She could see a glitter in the dark eyes, a lurking devilment that warned her of real as yet unspecified dangers ahead. She felt the muscles of her stomach tighten instinctively as he continued smoothly, 'That's very interesting, *mignonne*, but quite beside the point, since here, in Morocco, our marriage is perfectly legal until I wish to dissolve it.'

'Then do so.' She shrugged her shoulders dismissively, but the feeling of wariness lingered.

'I may do ... eventually.'

Now the amusement in his eyes transferred itself to his mouth as his lips twisted into a mocking smile.

'Karim ...' Vida swallowed, suddenly very much afraid of the ways things were going.

'Don't interrupt me,' he reproved gently, and now there was an element in his deeply evocative voice that sent a spine-tingling tremor through her. 'I've planned this reunion very carefully. I mean to keep you here in my sight until I tire of seeing your lovely, cheating face. Until the sunset in your hair bores me and I no longer thrill to see the dawn on your lips ...'

'The Lady at the Fair ...' Bemused by the low intensity of his husky words, she admitted spontaneously her recognition of the quotation.

'You remembered?' For a fleeting instant the smile he bestowed on her showed genuine pleasure. 'Yes, the Lady at the Fair, who turned every man's head with her beauty.' He continued to watch her with half-closed eyes as she shook her head in hopeless resignation. 'All my life I've collected beautiful things and never required them to give me anything but the joy of looking at them.' He smiled gently. 'An empty ornament, a two-dimensional picture—they satisfied my sense of beauty, my sense of touch.' He paused while his enigmatic glance followed the shape of her body before returning to the classical lines of her pale face. 'I was wrong to expect anything more from a woman.'

'You were wrong to dismiss the possibility so readily!' Vida flung back, roused from her lethargy by his cynicism.

'You have no need to keep defending yourself.' Strong shoulders moved in a negligent shrug. 'I admit during the first weeks in hospital I wanted nothing better than to kill you for what you'd done. Happily for you that feeling has now passed. You have little to fear from me now.'

Karim's casual dismissal of his earlier homicidal desires was hardly conducive to her peace of mind. With sinking heart she said quietly, 'Obviously there's nothing more to be gained from continuing this discussion. The sooner I leave the better.'

'You haven't understood me, Vida.' The expression on Karim's face shook her to the core with its purposefulness. 'There's no possibility of your running away from me this time. The British passport you travelled on has been taken care of.' He watched her eyes widen in horror as she remembered how she had handed over her luggage to Khalil. 'You are certainly legally married here and subject only to me. Believe me, you're not going anywhere until I've finished with you!'

She had to be calm. He couldn't really mean to keep her a prisoner, and with what purpose? It was clear he regarded her with scorn and bitterness. He was trying to frighten her. That he was succeeding was something she didn't intend to display.

Desperately she passed her tongue over her warm, dry lips. 'You've just told me I've nothing to fear from you,' she reminded him quietly. 'Now you're threatening to hold me here as a captive?' Colour flooded her pale cheeks as the precariousness of her position registered.

The cruel smile he turned on her before sweeping his eyes around the beautiful room promised her no

respite. 'It's a prison many women would sell
themselves for, and we both know you're no exception
when it comes to putting a price on yourself.'

The only price she had ever put on herself was love,
Vida thought bitterly, and that was one price Karim
had no intention of paying!

He was regarding her now with a speculative look,
eyes narrowed, mouth tightened. 'Or is it perhaps the
gaoler himself you find revolting?'

This was getting worse! What answer could she
possibly make to that suggestion? 'Karim, please . . .'
she begged.

'Please what?' he jeered. 'Don't tie you to a man
who's unable to be a real husband to you? Is that it,
Vida? What has your idea of living the life of a single
woman in London been, I wonder? Have I beguiled
you away from a lover with my promise of riches? Is
your body already missing his caresses?'

Dumbly she shook her head, refusing to rise to his
taunts. She watched his strong fingers grip the arms of
the chair, the knuckles whitening, compassion for
what he had lost welling like a deep spring deep inside
her. 'Because if that's what's worrying you, I can put
your mind at rest now,' he continued, his voice
rasping. 'I have several plans for your immediate
future, and I can assure you that celibacy isn't
amongst them!'

His words affected her like a body blow, knocking
the air from her lungs as he swung the chair away from
her, moving it with urgent hands across the room to
where a bell cord hung discreetly in a corner. Seizing it
roughly, he transmuted his feelings into a vociferous
summons.

Whatever did he mean by that last statement? Vida

sought desperately to find the words to question him further without betraying her sense of desperate unease. But before she could phrase her uncertainty a Moroccan servant entered the room, wearing a loose brown robe, his head turbanned in white.

Without turning, Karim sensed his presence. In the few moments that had passed he had gained control over his voice, speaking now in a calm authoritative manner. 'As you can see, Ahmed, my wife has now returned to live with us. I've arranged for her to be given the Harem suite. Please take her there and see she has everything she needs.'

The Harem suite? Vida glanced wildly towards Karim's implacable back. The Villa itself had four bedroom suites and she had assumed she would be staying in one of those. The Harem suite was in a separate wing, built round its own small courtyard, entirely self-contained. The Villa had originally been designed by a wealthy Arab who had believed in keeping the women of his family separated from the men in the age-old Islamic custom. Karim had once told her he found it useful when he himself was entertaining Moslems from the Arab world who adhered to the old customs and who travelled with their womenfolk.

Whatever his motives for accommodating her away from the main building, Vida was grateful. The greater the distance between them in this icy emotional climate the better she liked it!

'Well!' he snapped suddenly, forcing the chair round with a powerful tension of his muscular shoulders. 'Don't you see Ahmed is waiting?' He added as an afterthought, 'Dinner is served at eight-thirty.'

Somehow she dredged up her courage, determined not to let him see how shaken she was by his threats. 'Do I come here?' she asked, her chin raised at his eloquently lifted eyebrows. 'Or is it your intention to keep me in *purdah* and force me to eat alone?'

'You find the prospect of your own company daunting?' He had changed from French into speaking English, presumably so Ahmed wouldn't understand their altercation.

'On the contrary, at the moment I find it far pleasanter than yours!' Vida retorted bravely.

'In that case,' he told her, his mouth curving into a delicious smile that lightened the planes of his sombre face, 'I must insist you join my brother and myself at our table.'

Damn him for his perversity! 'And if I'm not hungry?' Every line of her rigid body defied him.

Karim shrugged easily. 'Then you can sit quietly while Khalil and myself indulge our own appetites.'

Their eyes clashed, hers flashing the blue fire of frustration, his mocking and alert, alive with an inner determination that boded her no good.

Karim was spoiling for a fight, she could sense it in every bone of her body. For a year his restless spirit had planned to avenge himself for the wrong he fancied she had perpetrated against him. She had walked a willing victim into his trap.

As the delicacy of her position registered, she uttered a long-drawn-out sigh.

'So bored already?' The teasing smile made her skin crawl. 'Well, make the most of your leisure. You may be grateful to have relaxed when you still had the chance!'

Filled with a nameless dread, Vida stared at the

hard-boned face of the man she had once adored, finding nothing in it to give her comfort. In that instant her stoic calmness deserted her. 'What do you mean? she asked shakily.

The reassurance she wanted was never given.

'Half-past eight,' Karim grated violently. 'And don't be late!'

She sprang back as he propelled the chair towards the open door, barking out a command in Arabic as he passed Ahmed.

'You will accompany me now, please,' the Moroccan said softly, speaking in French, his eyes cast respectfully on the floor.

She really had no option. Her head held high, Vida walked proudly from the room.

Following Ahmed from the main building, she walked through its cloistered terrace across the formal courtyard with its classic Moorish-style fountain. The beauty that had caught in her throat the first time she had seen it still had the power to raise her admiration.

Within the high-walled confines grew a sub-tropical garden of outstanding loveliness, shaded by graceful lacy trees including a few palms to remind her she was in Africa. Hibiscus, jacaranda, geraniums, hollyhocks, enormous cacti—all had evolved in a pattern of lush beauty that was even more breathtaking than she recalled.

Within the high wall at the far end stood a wrought-iron gate which she recalled led to the Harem suite. Mutely she allowed Ahmed to lead the way. At least if Karim intended to imprison her, her quarters would be luxurious!

The heavy gate swung open as the Moroccan stood back, allowing her to precede him. With a sigh, Vida stepped into the smaller courtyard and stopped, entranced. She certainly hadn't remembered these surroundings as being so well cultivated. Like the larger courtyard, this smaller enclosure was ablaze with splashes of colour between luxuriant vegetation, and the lily pond in its centre was surely new? As were the two large cages suspended from adjacent trees, each one containing a small singing bird.

It was a customary sight in Morocco and one which Vida still found disturbing, despite the fact that the birds would be attacked by their peers should they be given their freedom. Here, at least, the cages were large and well-hung and the birds trilling away in the cool shade of the foliage. She stopped for a moment to greet the small creatures in French, smiling at her own sentimentality. But they, to their credit, were apparently unique in welcoming her!

Ahmed waited patiently for her to rejoin him before continuing towards the separate wing and unlocking the main door. He stood back, bowing her across the threshold, indicating her case already standing in the entrance. 'I can send one of the girls to help you unpack, *madame*.'

'No, please don't bother!' She had brought little with her, not anticipating a long stay.

Ahmed nodded, muttering softly, 'As it pleases madame,' before turning and beginning to walk away.

'Oh, please wait a moment!' He turned an expressionless face towards her. 'You still have the key, Ahmed,' she said. 'I should feel much safer if I could lock my door at nights.' She held her hand out, waiting.

'You're quite safe here, *madame*.' He looked faintly surprised. 'The walls surrounding the Villa are much too high for a burglar to scale and the property is protected day and night by two guards who patrol the gardens. You need have no fear of intruders.'

'Oh, I see. Thank you.' She watched him go, unable to find the nerve to tell him the only intruder she was worried about was the man who claimed to be her husband. Such an admission would have achieved absolutely nothing. Here in this house Karim was all-powerful. She knew there was no one, not even Khalil, who would take her part against him.

Wearily she lifted her case and took it through the sitting room with its low couches and tables to where she knew the bedroom to be situated. The room was beautiful, furnished in shades of dawn pink and oyster, the floor of gold-veined marble, the curtains and bedspread of pure silk.

The bed itself was a double divan, and her heart gave a devastating leap as she recognised the white satin nightdress which had been part of the trousseau she had left behind on that dreadful night.

On impulse she went to the large fitted wardrobe which covered one wall, easing one of the doors open. There in front of her were the clothes she hadn't bothered to take with her—obviously well cared for, almost certainly recently laundered. She shook her head in disbelief. She had assumed Karim would have had them all thrown out a long time ago. It seemed he had always intended to engineer her return . . .

Slowly she pushed the hangers aside, remembering the joy she had had in buying the clothes, how she had looked forward to wearing them and seeing the admiration on Karim's face as he watched her cross the room towards him. She had fantasised about what would happen afterwards when they were alone in the master suite of the Villa. She swallowed convulsively as her thoughts echoed her dreams . . . Karim taking her in his arms, holding her body against his, peeling the dress from her skin and awakening her with tenderness . . . and love . . .

A small sob of despair rose in her throat. However desperate her own position, nothing could compare to the evil fate that had robbed Karim of his virility. If his mind was still warped against her, how could she blame him, when his vibrant male body had been dealt such an appalling blow?

Closing the wardrobe, she began to strip off her travelling clothes. There was little time before she was expected at dinner and there was nothing to gain by defying Karim's terse instructions on punctuality. She would shower, put on one of the summer dresses she had brought with her, and pray that after dinner his attitude towards her would mellow.

It was growing dusk as she stepped outside into the sweetly scented air. She shivered slightly as a cool breeze trembled against the skin of her shoulders left bare by the lowered shoulder-line of her dress. Her skin was still pale, opalescent against the deep rose pink fabric which was a perfect foil to her blonde hair hanging thick and slightly wavy in a curtain of silk to skim her back.

She had made her face up carefully, using only a minimum of cosmetics to bring its fairness into focus. The last thing she wanted to do was to draw unnecessary attention to her appearance and bring down on herself more of Karim's derogatory sarcasm.

Standing still for a moment, she inhaled the heady atmosphere around her, experiencing an unaccountable exhilaration. Above her head the darkening sky would soon be ablaze with countless stars. If Arab belief was to be credited her destiny was already written in the Book of Life. Not only was she Karim's prisoner, but the captive of her own future.

Her hands clenched hard, the fingernails digging into the palms as she stared at the arc of heaven. Fate or not, she would never give up the fight to vindicate herself against Tim Haydon-Smith's vile lying confession!

A slight sound broke her concentration, and her eyes blinked as she re-focused just in time to see a shadowy figure pass across the courtyard. Only too aware that the two guards who protected the Villa from unwelcome intruders would be equally effective in preventing unwilling visitors from escaping, Vida stiffened her shoulders bravely and made her way towards the beckoning lights of the Villa, her feet only slightly unsteady in their high-heeled sandals.

It was Khalil who rose to greet her as she entered the sitting room. Stubbing out a half-smoked cigarette, he came to his feet, according her a smile that seemed to sit strangely on his drawn face.

'You never used to smoke.' Vida eyed the ash-tray with its evidence of fairly heavy use.

'Since Karim's accident I've found it helpful,' he offered with a self-deprecatory shrug. 'It's been a bad time for all of us—Karim particularly, of course.' He seemed to find difficulty in meeting her eyes. 'Now you've come back to him, perhaps things will improve.'

'You mean when the divorce he wants has been established?' Vida's tone was dry, the anger scarcely hidden. 'That was the reason you told me he wanted to see me, wasn't it?' She refused to be placated by his

hangdog expression. Perhaps Khalil wasn't entirely in
his brother's confidence, but surely he must have had
some inkling of the way Karim's mind was working?

'Vida, please, you must try to understand how life
has been here . . . how greatly Karim has suffered . . .'

So he wasn't going to admit or deny anything!

'There are many different ways of suffering,' she
said stoically, letting her eyes rest disdainfully on his
youthful face. 'Mental suffering can be as hard to take
as physical pain, you know.'

Khalil's head rose sharply, an unusual arrogance
lending dignity to his expression. 'Something my
brother knows very well from experience!'

Immediately she felt ashamed. Karim's intolerance
had indeed reaped a bitter harvest. She would have to
accept that his manipulation of his younger brother
didn't reflect badly on Khalil himself, but was rather
an indication of the latter's devotion.

'Where is Karim?' She made no attempt to hide her
bitterness, casting her glance around the large,
elegantly furnished room, as if he might appear from
thin air.

'Waiting your arrival in the dining room. He asked
me to escort you.'

'Then we'd better not keep him waiting,' she said
with assumed brightness, hoping that when Khalil
placed a gentle hand beneath her arm he wouldn't feel
the nervous tremors that were plaguing her body.

'You'll forgive me if I don't rise to welcome you?'
Karim was seated at one end of the oval walnut table,
a cynical smile twisting the firm outline of his
sensitive mouth as he asked the rhetorical question.

Vida forbore to answer it, aware of and sympathetic
to the burning tension that had hardened his face and

tautened his strong shoulders beneath the fine, open-necked but long-sleeved white shirt into which he had changed. She saw the pulse throbbing in the firm column of his throat, betraying his aura of outward calm. Detest him and his uncompromising attitude towards herself as she did, she could still feel overwhelming sadness.

A quick glance round the room showed no signs of the wheelchair. He must have had it removed once he had been lifted into the dining chair. Here, at his own table, he could be an equal with his peers.

'Sit here, beside me.' He spoke peremptorily, indicating the appropriate chair. A flash of naked antagonism darkened the midnight clarity of his brilliant eyes. 'And save your pity for yourself—you have more need of it than I!'

Biting back an angry retort, Vida obeyed him. Despite everything her heart had ached for him, and he must have perceived something of her feelings before she had averted her eyes from his broken body. Clearly he found them unacceptable. Damn his pomposity! How she would love to knock that look of sneering condemnation off his handsome face. She busied herself spreading a linen napkin across her lap, pretending not to notice Khalil's embarrassment. Her erstwhile brother-in-law appeared to be even more nervous than she was! As the table had only been laid for three it seemed the forthcoming meal was going to put a strain on all of their social resources. Vida stared down at her hands. She had no appetite for food. How grateful she would be when the meal was ended and she could retire to the privacy of the isolated suite reserved for her use.

As Karim rang a small silver bell at his right hand,

she assumed correctly that it was a signal for dinner to begin, and steeled herself to face the endurance test awaiting her.

It was two hours later that she laid down her silver spoon in the accompanying crystal bowl, having finished a refreshing fruit salad. She had to admit the meal had been less of an ordeal than she had feared. The menu had been light, delicious and attractively served. To her surprise Karim had played the part of the affable host to perfection, demonstrating yet another facet of his complex personality. The conversation had been centred on topical, impersonal matters. For the most part she had been content to listen to the exchange of views between the two men, amused by Khalil's obvious gratification when his brother agreed with what he said, or accorded him a point, and oddly touched by what appeared to be the genuine deference Karim allowed the younger man's opinions.

On the few occasions she had ventured a comment she had been accorded a similar civility. She had been careful, though. She wasn't going to let herself be tempted too much by the mental stimulation she found from pitting her wits against Karim's. She was haunted by the feeling that his sudden affability was merely concealing a venomous desire to lash out at her once more. She had no wish to be humiliated in front of Khalil.

'May I pour you a coffee?' She took advantage of a lull in the conversation to address Karim, lifting the silver percolator the Moroccan servant had left in front of her.

'Do you remember how I like it?' The soft question surprised her, or rather the sudden intimacy of its tone as Karim's lips twitched in a half-smile.

'Yes.' Her monosyllable gave nothing away, least of all the sudden increased beat of her heart. Whether it was the effect of the light wine she had been drinking or the unexpected glimpse of the man she had once loved beneath the harsh exterior he had presented since their reunion she didn't know, but an unfamiliar warmth was pervading her body, giving her a sense of wellbeing that disarmed her defences.

Her hand shook slightly as she poured out the coffee beneath the cynosure of his gaze, adding a half-teaspoon of sugar before passing it across the few inches that separated them.

She forced herself to smile brightly in Khalil's direction, frankly disturbed by the light fluttering of her pulse. 'How about you?' she asked. 'Coffee?'

'I'm sorry. I have to leave . . . a party invitation . . .' He struggled to his feet, crumpling his napkin on to the table, looking gauchely uncomfortable as he darted a quick look at his brother's face, while studiously avoiding her own gaze.

It was the guilty turn of his head that confirmed her opinion that he was lying. He had been ordered to leave and he was obeying that instruction, however much he disliked doing so.

A wave of pure fear lapped down Vida's spine as the small hairs on her arms rose instinctively. She was being left alone in the Villa with Karim, as he had obviously ordained. Khalil knew what was in store for her, didn't approve of it, but had no intention of defying his elder brother's command.

CHAPTER FIVE

VIDA sat motionless as Khalil left the room, trying to take comfort in the thought that Karim might be about to flail her with his tongue—at least while she stayed to listen—but he could neither confront nor confine her physically. She had nothing to fear from a cripple. Again her mind winced at her own mental use of the word. It was the simple truth that despite the fact the threat to herself would be greater, she would willingly have faced it if the beautiful body of Karim Gavigny had been capable of functioning with its former vitality.

'Well now . . .' His voice, deep and melodious with a hint of a smile in it, assaulted her ears. 'I think this reunion calls for a toast in champagne.'

'Champagne? After such a splendid dinner?'

Vida deliberately forbore to challenge his suggestion that a celebration was called for.

'Champagne is appropriate at any time,' he replied easily. There was a pregnant pause that brought her unwilling eyes to Karim's watchful face. What she saw there made her catch her breath in apprehension. The set of his chin, the dark intensity of his eyes held a promise of retribution that reinforced his earlier hints. 'Especially now when we have so much to be grateful for—our first anniversary, the start of our long-awaited honeymoon . . . and of course . . . one more thing——'

Before she could react he had placed his lean hands

67

on the table and pushed his body upright before her amazed regard.

'Yes,' he said softly, his eyes never leaving her wide-eyed gaze. 'Yes, my beautiful deceitful wife, the surgeons gave me back what you and your lover so cruelly deprived me of.' The larynx in his smooth throat jerked convulsively. 'As you see, I'm no longer the helpless paraplegic you came so eagerly to visit. I'm as strong and virile as I was a year ago—but wiser and much more sceptical.'

Vida couldn't speak, couldn't find the words to express the overwhelming sense of joy and relief as Karim pushed the chair away from him and walked—yes, walked!—with his former grace and power towards the sideboard at the far end of the room. At that moment nothing could detract from the mounting wave of pleasure, almost ecstasy she experienced on seeing him move. Once she had loved him so desperately, so devoutly she would have offered her own life to a jealous God to bring about the restoration of the power of motion to the man she had married.

Pleasure flooded through her like a warm wave as he turned, a bottle of champagne in his hand, taken from the refrigerated cabinet—and faced her across the room. She felt humble and elated as if she were in the presence of a miracle, and her glowing eyes reflected her happiness for a brief instant.

It was only as Karim lessened the space between them and she felt the simmering passion behind his dark glance that she tore her mind back to the reality of the situation.

'You lied to me,' she accused dully. Then as an even deeper treachery occurred to her, 'Perhaps you were never paralysed at all?' All sorts of implications accosted her. 'You were never even injured! The whole thing was concocted between you and Khalil to . . . to . . .'

Remembering the look on his face as he had related Tim's false admission, she lost the power of speech. He hated her so much he had contrived to bring her back to Tangier with the sole intent of making her suffer! With a dreadful clarity she recalled his earlier innuendoes.

She searched his grim expression for a clue to his present intentions. His frowning contemplation offered her no mercy. Panic-stricken, she started to rise to her feet, only to be halted by his terse instruction, 'Stay where you are!'

The champagne bottle was placed on the table as she watched, trancelike, Karim's strong sensitive fingers encircling his own lean body, dragging the shirt from the snug belt that girded his hips.

'You require the evidence of your own eyes? Deny this—if you can!'

He lifted the shirt, baring the firm plane of his naked abdomen as Vida heard the painful pounding of her own heartbeats and felt a constricting pressure tightening her ribs. There had been a time when she had ached to feel that smooth skin lying like warm satin on her own tender flesh. She tore her gaze away, but not before she had seen the heavy pulse that throbbed between his ribs.

'Damn you!' he swore softly. 'You will look, Vida, if it's the last thing you ever do!'

Yes, it stung to be doubted, didn't it? Her eyes flicked back to his belligerent face. Once in the halcyon days of their short courtship he had returned from a visit to the local police station where he had been helping with enquiries, with a pair of handcuffs in his pocket. Playfully he had imprisoned her in a chair. She had never forgotten the feeling of total helplessness at being pinioned, entirely at his mercy. Then it had been a momentary act of teasing, ended before the rising panic had even shown on her face. Recalling that isolated incident, she couldn't doubt he would force her attention by any means at hand if she wilfully defied him. And this time he wouldn't be playing.

Too proud to answer him, she let her icy gaze rest on his body, her obedience to his command implicit. Slowly he turned, presenting the lean elegant length of his golden back to her appraisal. The damage, though not grotesque, was immediately discernible. Vida felt her mouth grow dry as her imagination filled in the details of the horror behind the flattened bones of his spinal cord and the silver line of scarred tissue that stretched from his centre back to fade into the hard muscle at the top of one lean buttock.

'So you sustained some kind of injury.' She hardly recognised the rasp of her own voice as she fought the hot curl of remembered loving that exploded inside her at his casual exposure of his firm flesh. 'Perhaps you were even paralysed for a time,' she conceded stiffly. 'But not when you sent Khalil to England. Why did you make your brother lie to me?'

Karim turned to face her querulous gaze as she recoiled from the terrible anger that illuminated the depths of his accusing eyes.

'As God's my judge,' he ground out harshly, 'if you want to leave this room with a whole skin it will pay you not to doubt my word! For six months I was confined to a wheelchair with no movement below my waist. It was as a last desperate resort that I was offered a chance by a specialist at the hospital in Fez. It seemed there was a slim hope that the spinal nerve had been pinched by shattered bone instead of completely severed.' There were tiny beads of sweat above his eyebrows and sudden lines etched against his cheeks. All doubt left her at the signs of remembered suffering even Karim's prideful self-control couldn't repress. 'The odds against a successful outcome were enormous . . . I was incredibly lucky.'

'I'm glad,' she murmured honestly as he uttered an abrasive laugh.

'Are you? Let's hope you feel the same way in a month's time!'

'A month? You expect me to stay here for a month?' A stab of apprehension lanced through her. 'I'm only entitled to two weeks' holiday. I hadn't expected . . .'

'To find me a man instead of a vegetable?' Karim finished the sentence for her with savage intonation. 'By heaven, Vida, you condemn yourself out of your own exquisite mouth! You were lured here with the promise of a divorce settlement, as I knew you would be. Why do you *think* I let you believe the injury your lover inflicted on me still incapacitated me?' The quizzical lift of his eyebrow mocked her silence. 'Because with all your effrontery I knew you would lack the courage to return to Morocco and put yourself in my power unless you thought I was incapable of dealing with you as you deserve!'

Vida swallowed painfully. This was far worse than she had imagined. Her initial happiness in finding Karim uninjured was now completely subdued, overtaken by a feeling of utter dismay and helplessness.

The gleaming smile on his saturnine face told her forcefully that not only had the full potency of his superb masculine body been restored to its former glory, but that he would have no compunction in using its regained power against her.

'I've already told you,' she said, speaking with tremendous dignity, 'I never wanted anything from you. I only came because Khalil persuaded me you knew the truth about what happened that night . . .'

'And so I do!' Karim had pushed the fabric of his shirt back into place and was intent on removing the wire from the cork of the champagne bottle. 'It's a subject I have no wish to discuss further—tonight or at any other time during your stay in my house.'

'Karim . . .' She halted, trying to conceal her nervous reaction. 'Karim,' she repeated his name a little desperately. 'I've told you . . . in England I'm not, have never been, married to you. You have no rights to keep me here. It's the simplest thing for you to get a divorce for yourself here in Morocco.' Her voice broke, only to be brought quickly under control. 'You've made it abundantly clear you despise me. What satisfaction can you possibly get from tormenting me like this?'

'The satisfaction you denied me on our wedding night, of course, *mignonne*, what else?' He didn't even look at her as he made the calm statement that took her breath away. 'You keep repeating what *you* told *me*. It seems you've forgotten what *I* told *you*. Here in Morocco you are most certainly my wife, and by the time I'm prepared to end that relationship, I can assure you you'll not need to be reminded of the fact.'

'No!' she cried fiercely, staring at the strength of his

purposeful fingers as they freed the cork, the power
latent in the strong thumbs as they pressed the stopper
upwards.

For the first time since the revelation of his restored
mobility she understood the full meaning of his
insinuations. Karim didn't intend merely to keep her
as a prisoner to watch and gloat over her helplessness;
he meant to mete out the punishment he had promised
her a year ago. He meant to humiliate and demean
her. Only now a year had gone by and she was harder
and braver than before. This time he had ensured she
couldn't run away, but by God, she would fight him
every inch of the way!

Her chin rose sharply. 'You're mad! Obsessed!'

'Insults won't make life any easier for you.' Vida's
breath hissed in between her teeth at his quiet drawl.
'On the other hand, flattery and co-operation might
ensure that you actually enjoy your unexpected
holiday.'

'You ... you fiend ... Ahhhh!' Vida's response
terminated in a piercing scream as the cork left the
bottle and flew to the ceiling, where it shattered one of
the light shades in a cluster of a dozen over the table.

Karim filled up two glasses to the rim before
surveying the damage, his expression hardening as he
glanced from the broken fitting back to Vida's
shocked and strained face. 'Your provocation spurred
me to the use of unnecessary force, I'm afraid,
mignonne,' he said with calculated irony. 'Still, if you
learn from that lesson the light shade won't have been
sacrificed in vain.'

He lifted a glass of champagne, holding it out to her.
'Now we drink to the start of our *lune de miel*.

Vida's eyes bright with tears of anger flashed with

barely controlled fury, as her arm itched to lift and send the glass crashing to the floor. For the moment she must let discretion overrule her valour. She dared only attempt so much. 'You must be mad if you think I'd drink to what you have in mind!' she flung at him violently.

'You may be right.' His smile was totally without humour. 'I was certainly mad a year ago when I believed you to be the innocent you claimed. I may still be mad to think that possessing your body will do anything to heal the pain that knowing you has caused me.' Darkly passionate, his eyes raked down her tensed form. 'On the other hand, you can gain nothing by attempting to prove your accusation one way or the other. Drink!'

On the point of refusing, Vida hesitated. She had always sensed a dark brooding side to Karim's nature: now his open aggression reinforced her fears. Something told her if she defied him he would have little hesitation in forcing the sparkling liquid down her throat.

Reluctantly she accepted the glass, to be rewarded by a smile of devastating sweetness.

'You learn fast, *petite*.' Karim raised his own glass and clinked it gently against hers. 'To the pleasures of the night!' He regarded her over the rim as he tossed back the champagne in one flamboyant gulp.

Because she had no option Vida sipped the cool liquid, her mind striving to devise a means of deflecting him from his avowed path.

Appeals to his mercy would obviously go unanswered. It was plain that for the past year he had been brooding on revenge for the wrong he fancied she had committed. And she *had* wronged him. Oh, not in the way he thought: but by running away instead of staying to face him at the time. She had loved him, loved the man she knew he had been when she had married him. *Then* if she had stayed, she might have reached through to him. Now, because of her original cowardice, she couldn't. The accident and her desertion together had transformed him into a monster intent only on reprisal.

'Finish your drink while I tell the servants they can retire for the night.' His peremptory instruction broke into her thoughts.

Watching him move effortlessly to the door, Vida obediently emptied her glass. Perhaps the simplest thing after all was not to oppose him, but to allow him the revenge he intended to extract from her unwilling body: not to prolong the agony by fighting him. He wanted his marital rights . . . so suppose she let him take them? He might or might not discover the evidence of her virginity. It wasn't a thing she would be prepared to bet on. Nowadays it was recognised that at least fifty per cent of women had no discernible barrier to cause them discomfort the first time they gave themselves to a man. At least tonight, with her senses blunted by wine, her emotions ravaged by the ordeal she had already been subjected to, she would be partially numbed to Karim's brutality. And afterwards he would let her go . . . Blunted by wine? Her pulse quickened as an idea was born. She had never been drunk, but reliable sources had told her it was like being anaesthetised. Normally she would have thought it the coward's way out, but nothing about her present predicament was normal. She'd do it!

Firmly she reached out, grasped the bottle of champagne and raised it to her lips. Swallowing deeply, she forced the fizzing liquid down her throat, gulping and choking as she prayed she could consume enough for her purpose.

The effect was instantaneous. She felt off-key, disorientated, slightly sick and—yes, numb. Gloriously, beautifully numb! She raised a trembling hand and pinched her own cheek . . . nothing! She took a few steps, knew she was weaving and that the vestige of feeling left in her legs was fast departing. The lights seemed unbearably bright. She peered towards the door through which Karim had disappeared, saw it open, sensed rather than saw his presence.

She moved towards him, her face burning, perspiration damp on her forehead and across the bare skin of her shoulders. Somehow she had to let him know she didn't care what he did to her now.

She opened her mouth, heard her own voice huskily deep and very, very quiet. 'Pleasures of the night,' she whispered.

The beautiful Moroccan rug was coming up from the floor to greet her, then it had disappeared and she was floating through the air, strong arms supporting her as warm sweet male flesh met her parted lips and her head nestled down on Karim's shoulder, her mouth touching the column of his neck.

She could feel the thunder of his heart against her own breast, and in that sweet instant before the darkness consumed her she knew that in the war Karim had declared she had won the first battle.

At first she thought the knocking had been inside her own head. Now, as she struggled to awareness, Vida realised that the series of raps had been on the door of her bedroom. She heaved herself into a sitting position. Dear heaven, her mouth had never been so dry in her life! Her tongue was cleaving to her palate and her throat felt as if it were lined with cement dust. She tried to speak, without success. Surely champagne didn't petrify the larynx? Resolutely she forced herself to swallow, found a modicum of relief, started to say 'Come in', then remembered where she was and changed it to '*Entrez!*'

Although the word came out as a croak it must have been loud enough to penetrate through the door, because it opened immediately to admit a young Moroccan girl bearing on a tray—oh, delight of delights—a jug of fresh orange juice, a glass, a cup and a percolater that brought with it the delicious aromatic smell of freshly ground coffee.

'*Bonjour, madame,*' the girl offered shyly. '*Il fait beau temps!*'

Vida smiled wryly as the tray was carefully laid on her bedside table and the girl moved to the window to fold the shutters back, exposing the open-grilled windows. Someone must have told her that Karim's wife was English and comments on the weather were the polite way of greeting the morning. Karim's wife! Vida flinched and clenched her eyelids against the sudden invasion of sunlight. She mustn't allow herself to think in those terms. She wasn't married . . . had never been married.

'Monsieur asks you join him for breakfast when you are ready. He will await you by the swimming pool.'

'Thank you.'

The girl gave her a shy smile. Through lowered lids Vida watched her departure before turning to the tray. It was then she saw for the first time that it also contained a glass of water and beside it two white tablets which were obviously aspirins.

The perfect host, she thought grimly, ignoring the water and washing the tablets down her throat with the ice-cool orange juice. Ah, what relief!

Her momentary surge of gratitude towards the master of the house subsided rapidly as yesterday's memories returned to her with a clarity that outraged and incensed her. All, that was, except what had happened after she had downed the greater part of the bottle of champagne.

Her fingers touched the white chiffon of the nightdress she was wearing. Had she really managed to undress herself and put it on? Her eyes, now accustomed to the morning light, surveyed the room. Not a sign of the dress she had been wearing—nor the underclothes beneath it! Subconsciously she could have followed the normal process of undressing for bed; certainly she hadn't been mentally alert enough to put her clothes tidily away afterwards.

That meant Karim had undressed her: divesting her of every shred of fabric before arraying her in the fantasy covering of the garment bought for her wedding night.

She groaned, swinging her legs out of bed and pouring out a black coffee with a shaking hand. Brief tracks of remembrance flashed through her brain: being in Karim's arms, the sense of motion and the cool breeze on her face; Karim speaking angrily and intensely in what must have been Arabic—swearing, perhaps? The softness of the bed beneath her, a cold wonderfully welcome compress on her forehead. She could recall how the cool water had trickled down her cheeks. She had tried to raise a hand to brush it away, but she'd been unable to rouse her arm to movement,

but it hadn't been necessary because . . . because . . .
She drank several mouthfuls of coffee, uncaring that
the hot liquid stung her palate. Was she remembering
accurately, or had she dreamed that Karim's mouth
had taken the drops of water from her face before
continuing to travel in silent salute to the warm nudity
of her uncovered breasts . . . and below?

Drinking the champagne had been an act of
bravado and defiance. She had dared Karim to do his
worst to injure her, and he had refused the challenge.
She stared thoughtfully at the dark liquid in her cup.
She had never received the physical expression of a
man's passion, but she wasn't so dumb that she didn't
realise that whatever liberties he had taken with her
helpless body had stopped well short of rape.

Finishing the coffee, she set the cup down gratefully. Already the aspirin was effecting its magic. Rising
to her feet she realised she felt surprisingly fit after
everything she had endured. A flare of real hope rose
in her. She had called Karim's bluff and been
successful. It was a fact that augured well for the
future.

Her step was light as she walked to the wardrobe to
select a cream cotton dress she had brought with her.
Yesterday she had been tired by the journey and
stunned by the series of shocks she had been given. In
retrospect she might have overreacted. Today promised her a far brighter future, she comforted herself
happily.

The garden smelled fresh and scented as she
emerged into its dappled beauty. Leaves of the shrubs
glistened with the fine spray of concealed water jets
and the small golden birds were singing their hearts
out as she reached them. Her watch told her it was

nearly nine o'clock as the soft warmth of the North
African sun caressed her bare arms. Turning into the
main courtyard, she crossed its elegant width, walking
on sandalled feet through the Moorish cloisters that
surrounded the Villa before reaching the pool area
with its raised levels and landscaped areas of statuary,
flower beds and shrubberies.

At the far side of the shining turquoise expanse of
water Karim awaited her. Vida stopped in her tracks,
surprised at the sudden surge of feeling that swept
through her. Beside a long low table bearing the
evidence of a Continental breakfast he was lounging
gracefully on one of two adjustable, upholstered
garden chairs.

Standing silent in the shadows, Vida drank in his
appearance: the strongly muscled legs clad in cream
cotton trousers, the brown and cream sweat-shirt
moulding firm wide shoulders, the strong sensitive
fingers turning the pages of a newspaper. A wave of
intense emotion flooded through her veins. Dear lord,
how she had adored him! With every fibre of her body
and every beat of her innocent heart she had idolised
this proud and autocratic Moroccan who had rewarded her by destroying the gossamer fragility of her
fantasy with a devilish brutality!

She had been little more than a child in an adult's
world when Karim had deigned to shower her with his
so-called affection. She swallowed down a sudden
lump in her throat. At the time she had really believed
he loved her, but all Karim Gavigny had ever loved
had been himself, and the reflection of that self he had
seen in her own limpid adoring eyes.

As for her own love—that had been real enough.
Even now the remnants of its painful disintegration

were like a poison in her blood, preventing her from finding solace in the arms of any other man. But that was a truth she would never divulge.

It must have been a sixth sense that alerted Karim, bringing him in a single athletic movement to his feet as he turned towards the area of her concealment. Reluctantly she moved forward, wondering what kind of reception she could expect.

'Did you sleep well, *ma belle*?' The polite enquiry was accompanied by a smile of lurking amusement as his lips curved entrancingly, displaying small grooves at their corners.

'Very well, thank you!' Unconsciously Vida's shoulders squared and her head lifted as she anticipated some cutting comment about her alcoholic state. When none was forthcoming she lowered herself on the other chair, sitting primly, her hands held loosely in her lap.

'Croissants, rolls, butter . . .' Karim lifted various covers, indicating that she help herself, before resuming his seat. Even if she hadn't felt starving the smell of the freshly baked croissants would have been impossible to resist. Taking what she wanted on to her plate, Vida was agonisingly aware of the amused scrutiny she was under from the man she had married. She might detest him, but at least she would show him she'd still got her manners!

'I have to thank you for having orange juice and coffee sent to me earlier,' she said stiffly, deliberately refraining from mentioning the aspirins.

'A courtesy extended to every guest in my household,' he returned blandly. 'Although your need was undoubtedly more desperate than that of most of my visitors.'

'Are you surprised, after the way you greeted me yesterday?' she demanded, stung against her better judgement into defending herself against his mockery. 'If that was an example of Arab hospitality, God preserve me from it!'

The look she received was quietly contemplative. Finding it more discomfiting than the acid retort she had expected, she looked down at her plate, busying herself with spreading butter on her croissant.

'Yesterday was a mistake.'

The quiet avowal stunned her. Karim apologising? A warm feeling of relief flowed through her. The bluster, the threats had been only to scare her after all; he had no intention of forcing her to consummate the illegal union she had entered into so blindly. Her breath escaped in a long sigh.

'It's all right,' she assured him quickly, generous in victory, anxious only to escape his unsettling presence at the earliest opportunity. She leaned forward in her eagerness, fixing his enigmatic gaze with earnest blue eyes. 'I'm quite prepared to leave as soon as I can get a flight.'

'When I say "a mistake",' Karim continued gently as if she hadn't spoken at all, 'I mean it was a mistake to attempt to force you into submission.' Happily Vida nodded her acquiescence. 'The only excuse I can offer is that seeing my wife again after such a long absence was more traumatic than I had envisaged. I had less control over the forces of resentment and rage than I'd credited myself with.' He bit his lip reflectively. 'I shall try not to repeat that error in the days ahead.'

Vida felt the blood drain away from her face, leaving her feeling dizzy. His reply warned her she had been too optimistic, too trusting—and why did he keep insisting she was his wife? Hoping against hope, she asked falteringly, 'You do mean to let me return to England, though, don't you?'

'Eventually.' The terse reply gave her no comfort at all.

'I don't understand . . .' The croissant crumbled into warm flakes beneath the sudden pressure of her fingers.

'Neither do I entirely, but the truth is that although I have no illusions left about you, I still desire you, want to possess you completely—and for all your duplicity I don't think you'll deny my right to take what is morally mine.'

'Then nothing's changed!' she flared back, swamped by a feeling of utter helplessness.

A slight smile twisted his lips. 'The only thing that has changed is that I am no longer content to have your unwilling participation—I want your co-operation.'

He had to be joking—only she knew too well he wasn't! He actually hoped, believed that she would willingly let him make love to her? To allow him to lay so much as a finger on her would make a travesty of the word. Before she could voice her angry protest Karim forestalled her. 'Don't pretend to be horrified. You know as well as I do the way your body quickened to mine in the past, responded to my touch when you were hell-bent on deceiving me. Your professed love was a mirage, but your arousal at my hands was genuine enough.' He gave a harsh laugh. 'I could have taken you at any time if I hadn't paid you the compliment of preserving your falsely-claimed virginity for our wedding night.'

'How dare you!' Vida flung violently, springing to

her feet and glaring down at him, her cheeks scarlet as she admitted to herself the truth of his allegation. She would have withheld nothing of herself from him. 'Whatever I felt for you then is nothing to the way I feel for you now. I—I despise and detest you! What sort of man is it who resorts to lies and deceit and prevails on his younger brother to uphold his treachery?'

'A patient man, *mignonne*.' The sardonic retort made Vida drew in her breath in exasperation. 'One who has spent a long year of pain and despair dreaming of what might have been—and what might still be salvaged from the wreckage of his dreams. And as for deceit and treachery . . .' he regained his feet languidly, but the expression on his face promised her no pity, 'I, at least, have the grace to admit it.'

'You . . .' Vida sought for words to express her contempt. 'You egocentric brute, you . . .'

'Enough!' Her shoulders were held in a firm grip as Karim glared down from his superior height. 'There is nothing to be gained by an exchange of insults. Face up to reality, *ma femme*. You're back where you belong. Let's have no more accusations about the past. Today is the beginning of a new chapter in our lives. Relax—you might even enjoy it!'

Too angry to be cautious, Vida raised her fists to hammer on the lean hard chest of the man who clasped her so resolutely.

'I'll never, never co-operate with you!' she cried vehemently. 'If that's what you're waiting for I shall die your prisoner!'

'A thought that wouldn't disturb me—even if I hadn't already received confirmation that it's only your pride that prevents you from surrendering without a token fight.'

'Token!' she gasped, affronted to the point of near-hysteria.

'Last night,' Karim told her with a sudden savage emphasis, 'I could have taken you with no resistance offered. In fact you begged me to. Oh, not vocally,' he taunted softly, 'but with every movement of your luscious body as I stripped away each flimsy covering that hid its beauty. In fact,' dark eyes glittered mockingly into her beautiful face, flushed now in aching embarrassment, 'can you be so sure I haven't already taken the first instalment of what I'm owed?'

She hadn't dreamed those intimate embraces, then. Her traitorous body had betrayed her after all. Struggling fiercely to free herself from his unrelenting grip, Vida felt hot tears gather behind her eyelids. 'Yes, I can be sure! I would have remembered *that*!'

'Thank you,' he drawled. 'You flatter me, *petite*. I promise to try and live up to your expectations when the time comes.'

He'd deliberately misunderstood her, and she wasn't going to give him the satisfaction of rising to his bait! The grasp on her arms lessened.

'Now we understand each other, Vida, sit down and finish your breakfast.'

'It would choke me!' she flung her refusal at him defiantly, refusing to be cowed by his domination.

'And if you continue to oppose me I may do so instead!'

Once there had been another man of legend. He, too, had been Moorish, and in an agony of misunderstanding and hate he had killed the woman he called 'wife'. A shudder convulsed her. She had no wish to play Desdemona to Karim's Othello. To pit her physical strength against the tuned bone and muscle of her self-termed husband would avail her nothing. There had to be another way of keeping her dignity and integrity. Please God she would find it soon.

Without another word Vida re-seated herself and began to eat with an unsteady hand.

CHAPTER SIX

VIDA finished her breakfast in silence, determined not to be the first to re-open the conversation. She had no weapons against Karim's implacability—even the truth fell wounded against the harsh exterior he had assumed.

Conscious of his contemplative appraisal, stoically she kept her eyes upon her plate. She wasn't unsympathetic to the trauma he had undergone. She didn't need a vivid imagination to understand the horror he had lived through. It was a pity, she thought rebelliously, he wasn't prepared to extend his own understanding to what she claimed to have suffered—instead of condemning her out of hand!

She pushed her empty plate away with an angry gesture that illustrated her frame of mind as clearly as words.

'Such fervour!' Karim muttered jeeringly, leaving her in little doubt he'd guessed the direction of her antagonism. 'And now you can tell me how you would like to spend the rest of the day.'

She could certainly tell him how she *didn't* want to spend it—in his company! She allowed caution to control her guarded response.

'Am I to be left to my own devices?'

'On your honeymoon, *mignonne*? Hardly.' A wicked humour lurked behind his narrowed eyes. 'Fortunately during my enforced absence from business my Uncle Fuad proved an admirable administrator. He can certainly hold the reins while I celebrate the return of my wife by devoting my time to her pleasure.'

Vida made a determined effort to ignore the repeated references to 'honeymoons' and 'wife'. They were deliberate goads and she would treat them with the contempt they deserved. It was just possible, though, she admitted grimly, that if he kept calling her by the endearment '*mignonne*' she might scream!

'Then I'm sure you already have your own plans,' she told him, tartly, meeting the gleam in his brown eyes with a challenge of her own.

Karim gave a lazy shrug. 'You won't want to exert yourself so soon after your journey. I thought we could take a picnic and drive along the road past Cap Spartel towards the Caves of Hercules.'

Vida would far rather have driven to the airport, but refrained from commenting on something he already knew. 'Do you still have the Khamsin?' she asked instead.

'I seem to remember you were impressed with it,' he commented as he nodded his affirmative.

Vida moved her shoulders lightly. 'Who wouldn't be? It's beautiful as well as functional.'

'A costly indulgence, but its performance justifies its expense,' Karim told her softly. 'I've always been prepared to pay well for service.'

The lazy way in which his eyes travelled over her from top to toe, taking in every part of her anatomy, flustered her as she was sure he had meant it to. She forced herself to return his impertinent regard with a cool smile.

'Then by all means, let's picnic. At least it will be preferable to being kept a prisoner in the confines of this place!'

'I remember a time when you expressed the opinion it was Paradise on earth.' Karim's expression held cynical amusement as he surveyed her set face.

'Until I discovered it was inhabited by a cruel, uncaring insensitive monster!' Vida had been caught on the raw by his reminder of her youthful naïveté: angry that such recollections spoken in his deep tones still had the power to hurt her so deeply.

There was a formidable silence as the humour died from Karim's countenance. Resolutely she continued to face him, amazed at his power to provoke a level of rage she had never known she possessed. When he rose leisurely to his feet she reacted too slowly to avoid the hand that reached down to drag her reluctantly up to his own level.

'I think you forget the requirements of the rôle you entered into so willingly a year ago,' he told her softly. 'It will be in your best interests if I remind you of them now, before Fuad and Laila return here from Marrakech and before you vent your newly found temper on my brother.'

'Don't bother!' she snapped back, her voice shaking with more rage than fear at his chauvinistic attitude. 'I recall very well what you expected—respect and service, wasn't it?'

'That's right.' His lean fingers tightened on her arm as he continued levelly, 'And I expect the same courtesies extended to my family and my guests. Whatever grudges you imagine you have against either myself or Khalil will be suppressed if you wish your stay in Tangier to be pleasurable and profitable.'

'Bribery?' she gave vent to a bitter laugh. 'But you needn't worry about Khalil. He was your brother before he was my friend and I can forgive him his deception. I realise he acted on a sense of misguided loyalty.'

'How strange that *you* are able to recognise such a quality.' There was danger in his taut disciplined body and the hard inexorability of his firm-jawed face. It took every effort of her willpower, but she refused to let her gaze drop from his accusing stare. He might well take her silence as dumb insolence, but if she attempted just once more to justify herself she'd dissolve into tears of frustration, she just knew it!

'No sharp reply?' Karim taunted sarcastically. 'Are you learning at last the wisdom of silence? It certainly becomes you better than the waspish retorts that have been springing so easily to your tongue.' His pompous approval was more galling than his scorn and the withering glance Vida laid on him was intended to leave him in no doubt of that fact. 'Tch, tch,' he chided, the sudden narrowing of his eyes acknowledging her unspoken message, 'a spirited mare is always a pleasurable mount for a courageous man, but you'd do well to remember that a fractious jade brings only the lash upon herself.'

'A colourful comparison.' Vida lifted her darkened eyebrows in mocking admiration. 'Apart from all the other threats you've taunted me with, do I take it you're now trying to intimidate me with the promise of a beating?'

'There are easier ways of silencing a rebellious woman, *mignonne*!' His hand reached out, entwining in her long hair, forcing her head backwards. Outraged at being so easily imprisoned, Vida opened her mouth to protest, but her words were stillborn as Karim's mouth descended ruthlessly, taking her own with contemptuous, rapacious ease.

She couldn't breathe or think as he took a devastating toll from her. Her fingers clawed at his shoulders as her legs buckled beneath his pitiless assault. Supporting her back with his other hand, he tightened his hold on her head, forcing it even further back so that her spine arched and her breasts were crushed against his chest as he leant over her, his face blotting out the daylight. She closed her eyes, enduring what she had no chance of halting.

Slow tears trickled down her face as he released her. She could hear the painful sawing of his breath, sense that he had received little satisfaction from the punishment he had inflicted, but couldn't raise her eyes to look at him. He had wanted to hurt her and he had succeeded. Not physically, although it would be some time before her mouth would lose the sensation left by its plunder.

Karim could have wounded the soft tissue he had held at his mercy: instead he had injured something far more precious. He had resurrected her memories of their love and systematically destroyed them, offering brutality instead of tenderness, power instead of pleading and selfishness instead of seduction. His savage action had killed any vestige of hope she might have nurtured of the qualities she had loved and admired in him surviving the cataclysmic experience he had undergone.

Mindlessly she caressed her own aching flesh where his fingers had punished her, stumbling a little as she strove to increase the distance between them.

'At least I think we understand each other now.' His steady tone showed not a trace of remorse. 'Behave with the dignity I require in a wife and you'll come to little harm in my care.' She wouldn't dignify the

comment by replying to it. Steadfastly she kept her
eyes fixed to the ground, schooling herself not to brush
away her tears. With a bit of luck he wouldn't have
seen this, her final humiliation. She heard Karim sigh
before he changed the subject as if nothing had
happened between them. 'I suggest you wear a
swimsuit under your dress. You'll find the Atlantic
makes a refreshing bath in the heat of the day. I'll see
you back here in half an hour—that should be long
enough for you to get ready.'

He turned abruptly without waiting for her agreement and moved with slow easy grace towards the
Villa.

Left alone, Vida clenched her fists. If only her own
good manners would actually allow her to behave
abominably in front of his friends just to shame him!
It would be worth enduring his anger to get the
satisfaction of making him lose face. Of course it was
impossible. It would mean humiliating herself. As far
as Karim's family and friends were concerned she
would be the very epitome of grace and culture. As far
as Karim himself was concerned, she determined
darkly, he would only receive her service and respect
when he deserved them!

She had brought one swimsuit with her. Stripping
naked in the privacy of her bedroom, she stepped into
the simple one-piece, smoothing it upwards over her
waist and breasts. Basically black with cleverly placed
white piping emphasising the shape and contour of
her breasts and the slenderness of her waist, it was an
elegantly designed garment and one she had been
unable to resist at the January sales in London's Bond
Street. Certainly, she thought with grim triumph, it
was a great deal more modest than most of the

beachwear flaunted on international beaches. There was no way she would have appeared in front of Karim half-naked in a bikini in his present frame of mind.

Grabbing her hair with angry fingers, she confined its loose tresses into a ponytail before twisting it into a topknot with a couple of hairgrips. Carefully she rubbed a high-factor sun milk into the exposed skin of her face and body, paying extra attention to her nose and shoulders. There, she thought with satisfaction, capping the bottle and leaving it on the dressing table, *that* would prevent Karim from offering to oil her! It was one of the oldest gambits in the business, and she certainly wasn't going to invite the touch of his fingers on her naked skin.

He was waiting in the little courtyard as she emerged after having covered her swimsuit with a scarlet towelling dress and slipped her feet into rope-soled, straw sandals.

She had deliberately kept him waiting to try his patience in payment for the peremptory way he had ordered her obedience. Consequently she made no apology as she moved languidly towards him, stopping purposely on the way to utter a few cooing words to the tiny birds in their cages.

'I began to think you'd changed your mind, *ma femme*. Two more minutes and I was coming inside to find out what was delaying you.'

'Why, Karim,' mock surprise coloured her reply as she fluttered her darkened eyelashes at him, veiling the glint of annoyance conjured up by his insolent appraisal, 'what else should I be doing after such a pointed reminder of my so-called wifely duties? I was making myself beautiful for you, of course!'

'Of course!' He'd been stung by the burning sarcasm as she had intended. Before Vida realised his intention he had reached forward to seize the tag of the zip on her dress and yank it downwards, so the curves of her swimsuit-clad body thrust through the gap in the towelling.

'You swine!' It was the casual violence of the act more than anything that infuriated her. The fact that she was perfectly respectable, and that Karim had known she would be, had nothing to do with the proprietorial way he had dared to assume the right to strip her.

She felt herself trembling with incoherent fury mingled with a rising hysteria. Of all the things to call a man whose admiration and respect for Islam was in no doubt—she had insulted him by referring to him as a pig! It would have been laughable if it hadn't been so terrifying, and if she hadn't felt every nerve in her body raise a pitch.

Quickly she gathered the edges of the dress together, stooping to reach the zip and restore her own modesty.

'Outraged virtue?' There was a hint of laughter in the question. 'My dearest Vida, I was merely confirming your assertion, and let me remind you I have already seen you without the camouflage of clothing . . .' he paused letting the import of his words sink into her consciousness, where they lay like a dead weight, before adding in a deceptively gentle tone, '. . . and have every intention of doing so again in the near future. Come . . .' He held out a hand, palm down, inviting her to reach out and grasp it. 'We've delayed long enough. The picnic hamper's stowed away in the car. Let's go!'

'I—I don't want to go anywhere with you.' The words stumbled from Vida's dry lips as Karim emitted an exaggerated sigh.

'Once,' he said softly but with an undercurrent of venom she couldn't miss, 'your every wish would have been my command. Once, when I believed you fresh and innocent and honest, I would have laid at your feet and let you trample all over me. Now, now my little infidel, you can go down on your knees before me until they're raw, and I'll not listen to one word you utter.'

'What happened to your sense of fairness, Karim?' she challenged, knowing she was insane to provoke him but driven on by a mental frustration that gnawed at her reason.

'It died the night I saw my bride spreadeagled beneath her lover!'

Despite her resolve Vida stepped backwards from the naked anger flaming in Karim's eyes. But she had gone too far to retract. Useless to repeat the account of her own agony—Karim had long since shut his mind to the reality of that. Instead with icy bravado she asked, 'And *you* were so pure you felt you had the right to judge?'

Something darkened his eyes—hurt? Guilt? His voice was quiet and deep in response. 'I asked nothing I wasn't prepared to give. I could have forgiven you a past lover, but not a present one: not a man with whom you had planned a future at my expense.' Wordlessly Vida shook her head, wishing she had never embarked on such a stormy sea bestrewn with rocks. 'I could have forgiven you for not loving me. I can never forgive you for pretending that you did.' Karim's voice roughened. 'Once more you've trapped me into discussing what is best forgotten. Haydon-Smith is dead, you're my wife, the past is about to be re-written!'

Oh God! He was impossible . . . arrogant, uncaring, pigheaded and blind, blind, blind! She wanted to cry out, 'But I did love you, you fool! Enough to leave my home and to trust myself to an alien culture with you as my protector. I loved you enough to marry you under a legal system not even recognised in my own country. You are the betrayer, not I!'

With an effort she suppressed the desire, knowing its futility. Instead she told him coldly, 'Over my dead body, Karim!'

'Necrophilia has never been one of my vices,' she was told coolly, Karim's composure appearing to be more easily restored than her own. 'Besides, if you want to return to your swinging singles life in London before the end of the summer, I imagine your self-righteous attitude will come to terms with reality.' He gave a meaningful pause, letting his gaze rove over her with studied impertinence. 'It's not as if you found me physically repellent, Vida. If you'd only relaxed a little more I think you might even have enjoyed the good morning kiss we exchanged earlier.'

Her eyes alive with sparkling fury, Vida bit back the bitter disclaimer that sprang to her lips. Oh, if only she could turn and run back into her bedroom—but obviously Karim would follow, and that was the last, the absolutely last place she wanted to take him. Neither did she want to spend the day alone with him at the Villa. God knew where Khalil was. In any case he would disappear at the flick of Karim's fingers, she told herself resignedly.

Still she stood rooted to the spot, unwilling to

accompany him.

'If you don't come with me this instant,' she was told levelly, 'I shall summon Ahmed and instruct him to pick you up and carry you to the car.'

He turned away, not even waiting to see her response.

He would too! Vida's hands clenched, the nails inflicting painful pressure against her palms. Any other man might have threatened to pick her up and carry her himself, but not Karim. Not the cruel, egotistical Arabian-Moor whose patina of suave French culture overlay a nature as cruel and unforgiving as his desert forebears. Not her erstwhile husband! Karim would summon a servant and have her lifted and stowed in his beautiful car as if she were a sack of potatoes or a lamb trussed up for sacrifice.

This time Karim had won. Silently Vida walked behind him, ironically aware that she was the customary three paces at his rear as behoved an obedient wife.

Seated in the luxury of the Khamsin, Vida maintained an air of quiet resignation. Beside her Karim was equally reticent as they took the road continuing through the Mountain, the scent of the pine trees resinous on the warm air. She was glad of the respite, temporary though she guessed it would be. She had never been the kind of person who could operate at such a continued high level of emotional expenditure without the strain showing. Driven as he was by dark forces of obsession, she guessed that Karim's capacity to inflict and endure the mental torture of which he was the progenitor would be considerably greater than hers. Although, to do him justice, if any shreds of the tender, compassionate and creative side of his nature, which she had discovered and loved, remained, he would not escape unhurt by his own bitterness. After a while, he flicked on a switch beneath the dashboard and the strains of Weber's clarinet concerto softened the area of unspoken hostility between them.

The gulf that separated them consisted of more than the misunderstanding, Vida reflected. Karim had diagnosed it himself, when he had told her that once her wish would have been his command. He had idolised her as if she had been a goddess instead of a real woman with human weaknesses. To Karim, the collector of beautiful things, she had been just one more thing to admire and own. In retrospect it was obvious. At the time she had been too overwhelmed by his interest, the intensity of his attention, to regard the situation other than through rose-coloured glasses. She had assumed they would always be happy. She on her pedestal, Karim protective and adoring at her side.

Sadly she reflected that even without the obscene, inexplicable action of Tim Haydon-Smith, their marriage would have had little chance of success. Inevitably one day she would have slipped from that pedestal—a word said in anger—a peevish, selfish response to some suggestion, bad temper . . . the list was endless.

Karim had never troubled to find out what she was really like—hadn't cared. He had seen the 'lily and rose in her face, the sunset in her hair and the dawn smiling on her lips', and that was all. He had been fated to be disillusioned. It had just happened sooner rather than later and in circumstances that made a mockery of justice.

Vida gave an involuntary sigh. At least Karim

would be in no doubt now as to the personality of the woman he had married. She couldn't help the corners of her mouth dimpling in self-mockery. Apart from all the frailties he wrongly suspected her of, he would know for sure she had a temper, a sharpness of tongue and a stubbornness that would be abhorred in a Moslem wife. It wasn't that she had deliberately hidden these warts in her nature, she justified herself, just that she had been too enamoured with Karim, too bathed in a cloud of euphoria for them to have been stimulated into existence.

'I imagine the quickest way to take that smile from your face is to tell you it makes you even more beautiful!'

Karim must have given her a sideways glance, but his eyes were fixed firmly on the road ahead, as he spoke.

Vida let her eyes rest on his classic profile: the straight nose with its sensitive flared nostrils, firm rounded chin with a hint of a cleft, eyes deep set and lustrous beneath clean-cut brows. She lifted her gaze from the thick fan of dark eyelashes to where his soft thick hair, bronze-black, not straight nor curly but rather springy, softened the line of cheek and brow and masked the top of well-shaped ears.

She took the inventory slowly, knowing he was aware of her scrutiny.

'Do you still like what you see?' he asked casually.

It would be stupid to lie. 'You're a very attractive specimen of the male species,' she said stiffly, pausing before adding acidly, 'outwardly, that is.'

Surprisingly Karim turned towards her, his white teeth showing in a wolverine grin. 'Then we start on an equal basis, *mignonne*. I too find you irresistible . . . outwardly.'

'On the contrary,' she flashed back, feeling the colour rise in her face, 'I find *you* totally resistible. I need to feel more for a man than a physical rapport before I can . . .'her voice trailed away. The last thing she wanted was to discuss making love.

'Have sex with him?' Karim finished her sentence with a lack of finesse which made her wince.

'You used not to be so blunt,' she said coolly, trying to shame him. Instead he gave a harsh laugh.

'I've changed in many ways this last year—as you yourself appear to have. I think we can afford to speak frankly, don't you?' His hands on the wheel of the powerful car appeared sure and steady. 'There may be little love lost between us, but that doesn't mean there are not other levels at which we can meet with mutual satisfaction.'

Vida swallowed her chagrin. 'I believe there are establishments in Tangier which could provide you with what you appear to be looking for,' she told him disdainfully.

'No,' he shook his dark head calmly, 'I want a great deal more than the cold-blooded tolerance I can buy in a bordello. We both know that before you were stupid enough to spoil your chances of a wealthy settlement you were quite prepared to indulge my lust for your body.' His calmly matter-of-fact voice continued evenly, 'A few moments ago you confirmed that you still had a physical rapport with me. In the circumstances I feel sure we could re-create the sensual delights we shared.'

The smooth unemotional timbre of his proposal was as much of a goad as if he had shouted at her. Oh, he

was absolutely impossible to reason with! And how
dared he say she had admitted to finding him
physically attractive when she'd said just the opposite!

'My feelings have altered dramatically since then,'
she retorted acidly. 'I can give you nothing of what you
want.'

'Of course not,' Karim agreed with deceptive calm,
but his white-knuckled grip on the steering wheel
didn't escape her notice. 'Whatever favours you
allowed me to enjoy while your plans came to fruition
were always going to cost me dear, weren't they?' He
shrugged indolent shoulders. 'Fortunately I can afford
to pay the market price for most things I want. In your
case, *mignonne*, even more than the market price.'

'Just what are you proposing?' she asked tightly,
more to gain breathing space than because she wanted
to know the answer, which was already painfully clear
to her.

'Oh, just an old Islamic custom,' he confirmed
diffidently. 'When a woman pleases her lover he buys
her a gift of gold. The more you please me, Vida,
during your short stay in my house, the richer you will
be on your return to England. That way you will
receive your divorce settlement for which you came
running so eagerly. The only difference is that you will
have earned every penny. I think it's an arrangement
that will work quite well for both of us,' he ended
complacently.

'Well, we'll never know, because I've no intention
of being a party to it!' Hating his cruel cynicism, Vida
flung her rejection at him with a shaking voice. 'I
don't make love to men I despise!'

Anger had lent her courage but wasn't powerful
enough to prevent her from recoiling at the glimpse of

terrible fury in Karim's black eyes as he shot her a piercing glance.

'Very well. Just remember I gave you the opportunity to make life a lot pleasanter for yourself. If you continue to oppose me don't pretend to be unaware of the consequences.'

'How could I?' she spoke with bitter emphasis, turning distraught eyes to his bleak profile. 'It's not the first time you've threatened to rape me!'

For several moments she thought he wasn't going to reply; that her accusation had touched some remaining element of decency in him. Then without taking his eyes from the road he said quietly, 'A year ago, whatever the circumstances, whatever I said, I could not have hurt any part of your beautiful delicate body . . .' She swallowed painfully as the silence extended again. If only she had had enough confidence in the power she had held over him a year ago, so much might be different now. But she hadn't. Silently she prayed that compassion wasn't beyond him, even if justice was. Her prayer went unanswered.

'Now,' he continued with ominous calmness, 'you can no longer rely on my reluctance to damage something which is so irrevocably flawed.'

Oh, dear lord, why when she hated him so much had he still got the power to wound her? Vida raised her chin defiantly, hoping he wouldn't see the tears glistening in her eyes. She was fighting a lost cause, but she'd make him battle all the way . She'd offer no armistice!

'If I'm so unworthy, why bother with me?' she taunted. 'Send me back to England empty-handed and forget about me.'

'And why, my unfaithful wife,' Karim countered

evenly, 'don't you confess to the plot you and Haydon-Smith concocted between you? I would then have cause to admire your honesty, if nothing else.'

'Probably because the last thing I want is your admiration!' she exploded forcefully, hunching her shoulders towards him and staring sightlessly out of the side window, pretending she hadn't heard the soft, disbelieving laugh that greeted her outburst.

For the next ten minutes they rode in silence. It wasn't until the car braked that Vida realised they'd reached the wooded area which stretched behind the expanse of silver sand which followed the coastline towards the Caves of Hercules.

She sat motionless as Karim halted the car, alighted and came round to open the passenger door. Stepping out, she refused to look at him, turning instead to gaze out over the stretch of azure sea.

'So you remember it too, do you?' Karim asked softly as he placed a lazy arm round shoulders that stiffened in automatic reflex. 'This is where we came the afternoon before I took you back to the Villa and asked you to be my wife.'

Minutes later, running across the pale sand in her bare feet towards the white-spumed rollers, Vida admitted to herself what she had denied Karim the satisfaction of hearing.

Yes, she did remember every detail of that wonderful day. Nothing had ever equalled the perfection of those moments in her life.

She'd been crazy with love for the courteous, passionate man who had made her the centre of his universe. She had been prepared and willing for seduction for the first time in her life, wanting to give herself utterly to his pleasure. She had wanted to love and be loved by him with a singleminded purpose without pre-conditions. She would never forget how she had felt when Karim had offered her marriage. It had been the final proof that he felt more than desire for her. Karim had loved her.

CHAPTER SEVEN

VIDA caught her breath as the early summer coolness of the water stung her legs. Conscious that Karim was close behind her, she plunged onwards, absorbing the shock as the water rose higher against her slender body. What a fool she'd been not to realise she'd become just one more acquisition to add to Karim's carefully selected possessions!

She threw herself forward into the breakers, gasping as the water cascaded over her head, enjoying the stimulating force of the sea as it touched shore for the first time since leaving the North American continent.

Damn Karim and everything he stood for! Not only had he killed all the feeling she had once had for him, but he had destroyed her ability to give herself in love and trust to any man!

She left the water before invigoration became discomfort. Towelling herself dry on the sparsely populated beach, she could see Karim's dark head between the breakers as his strong arms clove through the water. For a few minutes she watched, fighting her memories of the past, then she turned and made her way back to the shade-dappled glade beside the Maserati.

It was a full ten minutes before Karim rejoined her, by which time she had replaced her towelling dress and started laying out the picnic from the basket in the boot.

Concentrating hard on the task in hand, she arranged containers of cold chicken joints, basins of salad, fresh French bread, wedges of various cheeses, butter in a cooled container and an assortment of fresh fruit including oranges, figs and grapes, only too conscious of Karim standing within feet of her clad only in form-fitting black swimming briefs which did little to conceal the hard firm lines of his vital body—the strongly moulded thighs with their elegant masculine grace, the wide shoulders with their deceptively muscular strength. 'Do you like what you see?' he had asked her, and she hadn't been able to deny that she did.

He seemed to be taking an abnormally long time in drying himself, moving the towel in leisurely application to his wet skin with all the unselfconscious grace of an athlete. Vida didn't have to watch this casual display of sheer masculine beauty or be impressed by it. She forced her eyes away, concentrating on the task in hand.

The food was delicious as was the white wine which accompanied it, served from a refrigerated container. As he had at dinner the previous evening, Karim made it clear by his attitude that a temporary truce had been declared. Too much the Frenchman to spoil a good meal, she decided a little wryly, but too much Arab to call a halt to the war of attrition he had declared.

'You're lucky with your domestic staff,' she remarked pleasantly, finishing her last mouthful and relaxing against the trunk of a tree. 'That was a lovely meal.'

'The Villa has been completely staffed for some time now. After my accident there was little point in altering the arrangements that had been made. It was conveniently laid out for the life I thought I was destined to lead. Since Khalil had completed his course in business studies and found himself a job in shipping in the city he's continued to live there as well.' Karim shrugged his shoulders. 'Despite everything it lacks, it's a comfortable life.'

Still clad only in bathing briefs, he rose leisurely to his feet and started clearing away the debris of the meal. As he turned his back towards her Vida found herself staring at the scars that marred the firm tanned expanse of flesh. She hadn't realised how intense her gaze had been until she was asked gently, 'You find them too disfiguring?'

'No, of course not!' She flushed in confusion. 'I was just thinking how very much worse it could have been. I mean, if you hadn't been able to walk again or . . . or . . . anything,' she finished weakly.

The faint smile that danced in the darkness of his eyes and curled the corners of his gorgeous mouth told her he had tuned in accurately to her thoughts.

'Ah, but I can,' he said softly. 'I can do anything I have a need to or a fancy for. In fact, because of the intensive physiotherapy I had to undergo before I felt restored enough mentally and physically to seek out my wife and arrange for her return, I am even fitter today than I was a year ago.'

The odds were that his statement was correct, and it gave her no comfort. His consistency of purpose had been one of the things she had admired most about him. He hadn't achieved his business success without a great deal of personal application. Always in the past, she knew, Karim had got what Karim wanted!

And that was a recollection she would have felt better without!

'I'm glad,' she said coolly, refusing to nibble at the bait he dangled before her. Deliberately she smothered a delicate yawn. 'If you've no objection I think I'll do a little sunbathing and perhaps take a nap.'

'Of course.' The charming smile made her heart leap unexpectedly. 'You're quite free to do whatever pleases you.'

A magnanimous statement that was as counterfeit as a twenty-five-pound note, Vida thought crossly, as she bestowed an equally false smile on his innocent face before rising to her feet. She half expected he would follow, but he stayed where he was, lying down in the shade of the trees with his hands locked behind his head.

After an hour in the sun, Vida moved cautiously back into the shade herself, far enough away from Karim to prevent the need for conversation. Stretching out on her towel, she allowed her encroaching drowsiness to take over. Soon she was enjoying a deep dreamless sleep.

Whether it was the strain of the past days, the effort of swimming against the turbulent water, the good food or the deep lassitude caused by the North African sunshine, she would never know, but when she awakened to the sound of her name being spoken softly and found herself staring with drowsy eyes at Karim's serious face suspended above her, it was as if she had entered a time warp. Nothing registered on her consciousness except a deep basic need to touch him, to claim him as her own.

She was drowning in the melting pools of bitter chocolate that were his eyes, drawn like a magnet to the soft questing beauty that was his mouth. Unerringly her hands lifted to his head, fingers combing through the still damp tendrils that clung to his forehead. Water glistened on the tips of his eyelashes, crested his cheekbones like tears. The illusion of suffering was so great she heard her own voice sigh his name like a lament—'Karim—oh my Karim . . .'

It was only when he moved to seize the soft flesh of her shoulders, drawing her upwards into his arms, that the spell was broken and she felt a paroxysm of shock convulse her.

Still struggling for full consciousness, she stumbled against him as he half-lifted, half-dragged her upright, enfolding her bemused body into the closest possible contact with his own wet form.

'Please . . . no!' she begged breathlessly, her hands slipping on his skin as her mind registered the fact that he had come freshly from the sea to where she'd lain in merciful slumber.

Karim didn't answer, just increased the firmness of his grasp so that her breasts quivered against the warm naked wall of his chest and her thighs became conscious of every hard inch of the muscled length of his.

As his mouth sought her with a purpose that allowed no denial her first instinct to oppose him died an ignominious death, the power of conscious decision lost. Burning and swift, his lips met hers with an agonising silent appeal for acceptance. He was no longer taking without consideration. With every tender movement of his lips and his body, every soft incoherent murmur, Karim was asking for her response, unleashing a coil of fierce need that had lain dormant since he himself had first awakened it . . . a lifetime ago!

She was dissolving, her limbs melting, her body a morass of sensation as her arms clung to him for support, her fingers seeking the soft darkness of his thick hair as he released her arms to trail his hands down the length of her spine in a devastating exploration that even the protective towelling of her dress failed to render ineffective.

She was blind and deaf to everything but the man who was bending her to his will, obeying a force as primitive as life itself as she surrendered to his caresses. She whimpered as he eased the zip of her dress lower, dipping his hand inside to release her breasts from the encasing swimsuit, and lowered his head to salute their pale beauty with a voracious mouth. Arching her back, she offered their proudly crested loveliness to his lips, taking as much pleasure as she knew she was giving.

The hot spiral of desire that was sharpening her senses, increasing the beat of her heart, was becoming impossible to control, yet she had to. This wasn't the man she loved: the tenderness, the delicately worshipping kisses had been assumed to confuse her. Dear God, how nearly they had succeeded!

Desperately she tried to dislodge his head—without success; he merely drew her tightly into his body, leaving her in no doubt as to the degree of his arousal. Her hands, panic-stricken, moved to his waist, pushing vainly on the satin skin. Mindlessly her thumbs dug into the muscles, moved lower and dug harder, self-preservation giving her a strength and determination she'd never dreamed of possessing.

She felt the sudden painful tension of his maltreated muscles as he lifted his head, and for the first time realised how close she had been to the heart of his injury. A wave of sickness at her own unwitting cruelty assailed her as she swayed in his arms, then Karim was drawing her head down to rest on his chest, and she knew her breathing was only slightly less laboured than his as the thunder of her heart echoed the heavy rhythm of his. For a frozen instant they clung together until the increasing shame at her own behaviour stimulated Vida into breaking the contact of their bodies.

Sun, sea, sand—all came into focus, replacing Karim as the sole occupant of her world as she lifted dazed, dark-pupilled eyes to scan his face, expecting—what?—contempt, triumph?—at her unconditional response in the wake of all her oaths of indifference.

He continued staring at her through half-shuttered eyes, his jaw relaxed, lips slightly open, desire lending his handsome face a terrible beauty as the needs of his body overrode the censorship of his mind.

In the heat of the African sun, Vida shivered. She had thought herself immune to Karim's fatal magic. How dreadfully wrong she'd been! Her only protection against his lust had been the lack of privacy on a public beach—even one so sparsely populated.

She fought down a feeling of total helplessness. Possession without love was as abhorrent to her now as it had been on the night she had fled, bruised and forsaken, from Karim's violence. It was something she must never let herself forget.

'It's time we returned to the Villa. Fuad will be back and waiting to see me.' Karim's voice was unsteady as he reached down for his towel.

'How will you explain my being here in Tangier?' Vida strove to make casual conversation—anything rather than having to analyse what had just happened between them. Besides, she had always felt at a disadvantage with Karim's so-called uncle. She knew there waa no blood relationship between the two men. Shortly after she had first met him, Karim had explained that the taciturn Arab was the brother of his paternal uncle's wife! The relationship was a tenuous one by Western standards, but Vida had realised that the strong bond of kinship which prevailed in the Arab world forged a link that was tantamount to an obligation. Besides, it was natural for Karim to want to keep in contact with a man who shared his real father's nationality, she supposed, and from what she had heard Fuad had certainly been there to help his kinsman in Karim's hour of need.

'What explanation do I need to give him?' Karim spoke curtly as he finished using the towel and slung it across his shoulder. 'You're my wife, as Fuad is well aware since he attended our wedding. Your place is in my home.'

'Until you decide otherwise!'

She couldn't help the bitterness in her tone, humiliatingly aware of her mouth still warm and used, its liquidity echoed throughout the other pulsating membranes of her pliant body that had yielded with shameful ease to Karim's nearness.

'Yes,' he agreed softly. 'Yes, *mignonne*, that is precisely it!'

Vida took her time preparing for dinner, trying to come to terms with her own wild behaviour on the beach and failing miserably. How on earth, with every reason to hate and distrust her former husband—now playing the role of captor—had she come to throw herself into his arms?

An even more unpalatable fact was the realisation that in that moment of total abandonment she had experienced a re-birth of the feelings she'd once nurtured for him.

Of course they had been an illusion, conjured from the past by the repetition of images deliberately presented to suborn her. Like a fool she had been swayed by the memory of that long defunct magic. It must never happen again, she told herself grimly. By Karim's own admission he was after her willing submission. Probably at this very moment he was congratulating himself on how well his ploy had worked.

Well, if he thought tonight would see her easy capitulation he was wrong. She would be cold and distant. If he attempted to hold her or kiss her she would stay dormant and unresponsive. She would remind herself of all the terrible things he'd said and done to her ... and force herself to ignore the unwelcome effect his nearness still had on her senses. The alternative was too dreadfully humiliating to contemplate.

Her heart leapt at the sound of gentle knocking on the outside door. Karim had come over to escort her to dinner? Incredulously a wave of excitement brought a flush of colour to her cheeks. She stole a quick furtive glance at herself in the mirror, recognising without undue vanity that her eyes were sparkling, her skin glowing and the veil of ash-blonde hair formed a dramatic contrast to the tobacco-brown silk dress she had chosen.

Carefully she composed her face and counted to ten before opening the outer door. Instantly the cool smile

she had assumed froze on her lips as she encountered
Ahmed's expressionless face. His eyes slid obliquely
from her face towards her feet in a gesture which
seemed sly but was, she knew, a token of obeisance to
her in her role as Karim's acclaimed wife.

'The master sends me to request that tonight you
dine here in your room.'

'Just the two of us?' she spoke unthinkingly. This
was a new hazard. She had anticipated dining with
Khalil and Fuad, perhaps even Laila. It would have
been very pleasant to have another woman's company. A dinner *à deux* was something she hadn't
considered.

But Ahmed was speaking as if she hadn't interrupted. 'He wishes me to explain that tonight he entertains
important guests from overseas and is unable to share
his company with you. Dinner will be served to you in
your room and the master wishes you *bon appétit*. He
feels sure you will understand and looks forward to
seeing you tomorrow.'

'Yes, I understand.' Vida made herself speak
calmly, waiting while Ahmed gave a little bow before
turning and leaving.

It took every effort of self-control not to slam the
door. Oh yes, she understood all right! She was fit for
his bed, but not fit for his table when he had important
guests! She gave a brief explosive laugh. She should
have expected something like this. In the game of cat
and mouse Karim was playing with her, his action had
the fine edge of a studied slight.

Footsteps on the path warned her of the approach of
one of the maids with her solitary meal. Sighing, she
bowed to the inevitable, standing back to allow the
girl to enter with a laden tray. But if she'd expected

bread and water or the Moroccan equivalent she was to be disappointed. The meal of melon, chicken à l'orange with fresh vegetables, cheesecake and fruit was well up to Cordon Bleu standards. In Vida's mouth it tasted as uninteresting as sawdust.

She ate as much as she could, read a couple of magazines which had been left on the table and decided on an early night.

There was something about the early African evening, its warmth and dusky sky, that intensified her sense of melancholy. She could recognise so many of the emotions churning inside her—anger, hostility, mental frustration. Today to the almost endless list one more had been added—a heartrending sense of loss. Sleep must be the answer. In the morning she would feel better.

She did. Awakening early, she was showered and dressed before her pre-breakfast tray was served. Sitting outside by the lily-pond enjoying the drinks, she was very much aware of her change of mood. This morning she felt restless and excited as if she was standing on the threshold of an adventure. To-day she would be a foe worthy of Karim's steel, she determined, and as soon as the right opportunity arose she'd leave him in no doubt at all on that point!

The pool area was deserted save for two male Moroccan servants intent on cleaning out the pool itself. Taking her time, Vida strolled through the graceful cloisters, stopping now and then to admire the high stone pots filled with a profusion of flowering colour.

She had expected Karim to be in the dining room, but it was Khalil who rose to greet her as she entered.

He looked uncertain and shamefaced—as well he might! Her undertaking to Karim fresh in her mind, Vida greeted him with a cool politeness.

'You must feel I owe you an explanation,' he said unhappily, reseating himself across the table from her as she sat down and helped herself from the plate of still-warm croissants.

'No.' She avoided meeting his troubled eyes. 'I understand that Karim's commands are law as far as you are concerned.'

'You think I wouldn't dare to disobey him?' The tone was all injured male, so much so she found it hard to hide the unbidden curl of her mouth. It was exactly what she did think.

'You're wrong,' Khalil said tersely. 'Naturally he has my loyalty, but I'd oppose him if I thought what he asked me to do was wrong.'

'Really?' She raised scathing eyebrows. 'So in your estimation, feeding me a pack of lies to arouse my pity; forcing me to return to an environment full of hate and distrust is a—a civilised action to take?'

'You came voluntarily!' Hot colour rose in his face as he sought to justify his lies. 'Karim loved you. He wanted you back where you belonged. He only did what he thought was necessary to bring that about.' This time he didn't flinch from her accusing stare. 'I think he was right.'

'Do you indeed!' Vida fought down an urge to lean across the table and shake him. 'Then you're very young and very naïve, Khalil. Whatever your brother feels for me, it certainly isn't love. I could give you many names for it—but I hesitate to embarrass you!'

His dark eyes flashed fire. 'I'm barely a couple of years younger than you ... and as for naïve ...' He gave a bitter laugh. 'I wasn't naïve when I sat by Karim's bed and watched him deeply sedated but crying out your name over and over again!' Silently she shook her head, denying love as the source of those cries. But Khalil was rushing on, words coming thick and fast. 'Perhaps it's *you* who are naïve, Vida. You're angry and hurt because he didn't get in touch with you after the attack, aren't you? You think Karim was sitting in a wheelchair nice and comfortable, waited on hand and foot with nothing to do all day. You think he should have spent his time writing to you, begging you to return, don't you?'

Certainly at the time she had resented Karim's silence. Now she knew the lies he had been fed she understood it. But unless she took Khalil completely into her confidence how could she explain her attitude? But Khalil wasn't even waiting for a reply.

'Have you any idea just how much my brother suffered in those early months?'

She looked sadly at his furious young face. 'Believe me, I don't underestimate what it must have been like for a man like Karim to be paralysed . . .'

She didn't have time to finish the sentence.

'Do you underrate the pain, then? The agony he suffered?'

'Physical pain, do you mean?' Now she was shocked. 'But I thought with paralysis there was no pain.'

'He was in pain all the time.' Khalil's face was set grimly. 'Sometimes it happens like that—just above the site of the injury there is constant searing pain. I've watched Karim, his face grey with the agony of it, fighting not to show his despair!'

'Oh God,' she muttered. Death had been too kind

an escape for Tim Haydon-Smith. She hoped unchari-
tably that he was rotting in Hell.

'It's not only being unable to walk either,' Khalil
continued doggedly. 'When a man's paralysed like
that he loses control of his bodily functions and with
that—his self-respect. Where his back and his thighs
are a dead weight, unless he is very careful, he gets
sores—deep, painful sores...' His voice broke and
she saw his lustrous eyes were bright with unshed
tears.

'Khalil...' Spontaneously she reached out a hand
to him, unable to speak for the tears choking her own
throat.

He took her hand, holding it tightly in both of his, as
he regained control of himself, and continued, 'You
know, Vida, when he was first sent back to the Villa,
when they thought there was no hope, Maman wanted
to stay here with him, but he sent her away. He said
... he said mothers were too possessive, but the real
reason was that he wanted to spare her the sight of his
endless pain.'

'But he let *you* stay?' she asked gently.

'I'm his brother and I'm a man!' The chin lifted
proudly. 'I think he enjoyed my company and also that
he wanted to show me that when suffering is
unavoidable then a man must accept it and live with it
any way he can.'

'He was very lucky to have you, Khalil,' Vida said
softly. 'You must love him very much.'

'It's not *my* love he wants!' The retort was trembling
with emotion. 'It's yours, Vida. The only reason he
fought against the odds so indomitably was so that he
could bring you back here. I'll never forget his face
when the surgeons offered him that tiny sliver of hope,

or how he looked before he went into surgery, because he would never have tried to reach you again if it had failed.' There was naked aggression on Khalil's normally gentle face as he released her hand with a gesture of disgust. 'And all the time Maman and I waited outside the operating theatre—you, his wife, were a thousand miles away!'

'Khalil, please . . .' She understood his rage, but sadly she recognised that he would find her explanation of her actions as unbelievable as his brother did. 'It's something Karim and I must sort out for ourselves. I don't expect you to like me, just . . .' She swallowed down her own tears. There wasn't much joy to be had from being surrounded on all sides by hostility. 'Just try not to hate me too much.'

'I don't hate you,' he said dully. 'I just hate what you did to my brother—what you're still doing to him.'

She shouldn't have expected a different reaction, Vida supposed wearily. If there'd been a happy reunion she would hardly be occupying the isolated little suite.

'Circumstances aren't always as simple as they seem to an observer,' she told him sadly.

'You think I don't know that?' To her surprise Khalil's mouth twisted into a wry grimace. 'I'm not so young that I don't know the problems that can exist between lovers.'

'*You're* in love, Khalil?' There had been such a wealth of meaning in his objection she could hardly doubt it. His friendship with Sara had been just that. Somehow she hadn't expected his emotions to have matured so quickly. Yet he had changed dramatically in the last twelve months and it would be churlish to underestimate his capacity for deep feeling.

'I can't deny it.' He shrugged his shoulders with a mock bravado that tugged at her heart. 'Unfortunately, her family are opposed to our friendship. They've already made plans for her. We can only meet in secret and then only at great risk to her.'

'She's a Moslem, then?' and as Khalil nodded unhappily, 'Does Karim know? Surely he can, and, would intercede on your behalf?'

'It's not as simple as that.' He waved aside her suggestion. 'Besides, Karim has his own problems. I can't add to those.'

'By that I suppose you mean me?' Vida asked drily. He didn't answer, but the rising tide of colour on his youthful face confirmed her suspicion. 'I doubt he'd thank you for fighting his battles for him. Believe me, your big brother has an armoury of weapons himself, which he's more than capable of using!'

'Oh God, Vida!' Long fingers laced through his tousled curly hair as he held his head in his hands. 'I don't know what came over me. I should never have spoken to you like that. Karim would kill me if he found out!'

'He won't from me,' she assured him with a slight smile.

Karim wasn't a man who would appreciate her discussing the pain and indignities he had suffered with his brother. She was grateful to Khalil, though. The added knowledge made it easier for her to understand Karim's desire for vengeance. Tim was beyond his reach, but in Karim's mind she bore equal blame for what had befallen him. The unyielding spirit of the man she had loved demanded that someone pay for what he had suffered, and who else was there? In the circumstances, she thought with icy detachment from her own fate, it was difficult to blame him.

'Where is Karim?' She tried to bring the conversation back to a general plane. 'Still recovering from the excesses of last night?'

'Hardly excesses.' With the natural resilience of youth Khalil's face creased into a grin. 'Moslem businessmen don't indulge in alcohol.'

'Of course,' she returned his smile with a lift of her eyebrows. 'Or the company of women either, it seems.'

'I was excluded from the table too, if that's what's worrying you.'

'No worry.' Vida dismissed yesterday's irritation airily. 'It must have been very confidential for you to be banned.'

'Yes.' He frowned. 'As a matter of fact I don't think it was anything to do with Karim's normal business. There were three of them, Arabs, not Moroccans— and Fuad, of course. He was the one who brought them. I have a feeling they were fellow-countrymen of his from Al-Khazar-ja.' He shrugged lean shoulders. 'It was probably political. It wouldn't be the first time, I think.'

'Really?' Vida accepted the cup of coffee Khalil offered her, intrigued by what he had suggested. She had never envisaged Karim being involved with Middle Eastern politics. But if the visitors had been compatriots of Fuad's they must also have been the same nationality as Karim's natural father. Also, of course, Karim was a wealthy man. What more natural than his being approached to give financial support to one of the many Arab causes? Such matters would be treated circumspectly and it could explain why both she and Khalil had not been welcome.

It took some of the sting out of her own rejection. It didn't mean, however, that her overriding attitude towards the domineering Moroccan had altered one whit!

'So he's just catching up on his sleep?'

'No. It seems he was up at first light and decided to exercise one of the horses along the beach before the crowds arrive. He left us a message with Ahmed.'

Vida suppressed a sigh. In happier times how she would have loved to have accompanied him. The idea, when it hit her, was nothing short of a brainwave. With Karim absent she had been given the opportunity to show him she was far from being subdued by his dictatorial attitude.

Controlling her rising excitement, she asked casually, 'If you're going to work in the town today perhaps you can give me a lift?'

'I was going to walk.' Khalil shot her a quick, concerned glance.

A small curl of triumph unwound in her heart. 'I'll walk with you, then.'

She kept her voice light, trying to make it sound the most natural statement in the world. She had a very strong feeling indeed that the 'Guardians of the Gate', as she had mentally termed the prowling Moroccan servants, would certainly prevent her from leaving unescorted. Khalil was a different matter. Provided she made the suggestion sound inconsequential she might just stand a chance of getting away with it. Something told her Khalil hadn't been told she was virtually a prisoner.

'I want to do some shopping,' she improvised wildly, adding for full measure, 'I really do need some comfortable sandals.'

'Karim will take you out shopping when he comes back.' He obviously wasn't very happy about the idea. Had there been a direct instruction given to ensure she didn't leave? Her quickened pulse thrummed like a hummingbird as she made a little moue of disappointment. 'That would be dreadfully boring for him! After all, don't forget I do know my own way about.'

Even outside the Villa her movements would be limited by her lack of passport and money. She would have to return in due course, she knew that, but not before she had shown her independence, her determination not to comply with Karim's autocratic rules for her behaviour.

She could almost see the battle going on in Khalil's head! Obviously Karim hadn't given precise instructions. After all, the role of jailer was not a particularly laudable one and he hadn't wanted to lower his image in the eyes of the younger man. It gave her a thrill of satisfaction to realise Karim's vanity could be used against him. It was a chink in his armour, and she could definitely use a few of those!

Pressing the advantage Khalil's hesitation afforded her, she went on happily, 'Oh, and by the way, do you know where Karim's put my passport? I shall have to change some travellers cheques.' Carefully she kept any hint of accusation from her question.

'No—no . . .' Khalil avoided her glance. 'That is—I expect he's locked it away in the safe in his bedroom.'

Damn! She should have thought of that. Karim often brought extremely precious items back to the Villa. The safe was impregnable and the combination known only to him.

Khalil, who had seen her face fall, added eagerly, 'Let me lend you some currency. I can manage the equivalent of about twenty-five-pounds if that'll do.'

'All right.' Vida smiled her thanks, triumphantly aware that the offer meant Khalil had decided in her favour. 'I'm ready to leave when you are.'

'You'll leave a note for Karim?'

He was still worried, as well he might be, she thought grimly. If he'd suspected just how outrageously his brother had acted towards her, he would have felt even more concerned! Still, she comforted herself, Khalil wasn't totally without blame in this bizarre plot, and the odds were that Karim would be much more tolerant of his brother's shortcomings than her own.

'Of course!' she agreed without hesitation, taking a pen from her bag and tearing a page from her diary as Khalil rose from the table and made for the door.

She took the greatest of pleasure in leaving the terse message—'Gone shopping', signing it merely 'V' before following Khalil from the room. Wouldn't she have just loved to see Kharim's face when he came back and found her missing!

CHAPTER EIGHT

IT was wonderful to feel free! Vida drew in a full breath of the sparkling air once she had bade Khalil goodbye and determined to enjoy herself.

With the whole day ahead of her to recapture the sights and sounds of the city she had grown to love but thought never to see again, she started the morning by walking down the Boulevard Pasteur, taking her time to admire the latest fashions displayed in the Moroccan fashion shops with their imported couturier designs from all over the world, relaxing over a coffee in a couple of the many cafés, lingering to watch the steady parade of colourful people from a multitude of races.

It was a pity, she reflected, that Greg was no longer in Tangier but had transferred his headquarters to Casablanca. How good it would have been to see him again. Perhaps in conversation she might have gleaned some clue to the ever-present nagging problem of Tim's attack. She supposed many of the acquaintances she had made in Tangier at the time would still be around, but then their meetings had been so casual it was unlikely if any of them even remembered her!

Attracted by the delicious smell emanating from a French bakery, she entered the beaded doorway, emerging minutes later with two salad rolls and a deliciously wicked calorie-laden cream pastry. Tension, she reflected ruefully, always increased her appetite for carbohydrate!

Making her way towards the Medina, she entered the Grand Socco—the main market place with its cafés fragrant with the scent of mint tea and its stores where spices shared space beside rolls of exquisite fabrics, and where a great crush of people in a fancy-dress array of costume jostled against each other.

Here there were dark-skinned Moroccans in robes and turbans mingling with women whose heavily made-up eyes stayed demurely fastened to the ground above veils which completely hid their faces, in direct contrast to the Rif peasant women down from the mountains in the typical dress of red and white striped apron over voluminous skirts, wide-brimmed straw hats decorated with coloured woollen tassels and leather shin guards to protect their legs from thorns; beautiful Moroccan women dressed in the latest European fashions walked with handsome dark-eyed men who wouldn't have looked out of place in London's Bond Street. Slender bright-eyed children abounded, and of course, there were the tourists, their motley assortment of dress ranging from shorts and mini-skirts to bare-chested men and scarcely more modestly clad women, accepted and tolerated in this mêlée of humanity.

Gradually Vida felt the strain of the past days draining away from her. Here amidst such a thriving mass of humanity she could relax, her brightly printed dress and fair hair only making a tiny addition of colour to the rainbow landscape. Her hand tightened on her handbag with a philosophy born of experience. Like any thriving market place, the Grand Socco attracted its share of thieves and villains!

The Mendoubia Gardens at the end of the Grand

Socco provided just the place she needed to eat her
lunch. Previously the residence of the Sultan's
representative, the gardens were an oasis of peace
with their foliage, pebbled paths and display of
seventeenth-century artillery pieces.

It was early afternoon when she made her way
leisurely down the Street of the Jewellers with its
myriad shops displaying the bright red gold typical of
the region, and the intricate hand-worked silver
mined in the Rif Mountains. Here too were the
antique shops and bazaars which were a happy
hunting ground for the initiated.

It wasn't a place Vida wished to linger in. Deprived
of her presence, who knew what Karim might do to
pass the time? It was feasible he might have business
in this area, and chance meeting with her tempera-
mental husband was the last thing she was looking for.

Automatically her steps led her towards the tangled
web of streets in the Little Socco. Here it was all too
easy for the unwary tourist to get lost. Fortunately her
own sense of direction allied to her excellent memory
gave her no reason for alarm as she wandered through
the intricate labyrinth, stopping to buy a few odds and
ends, including the sandals she had voiced a need for
and unable to resist treating herself to a delicate
filigree silver bracelet, fastened by the traditional
lucky Hand of Fatima. She could use a little luck, she
admitted wryly, tucking the carefully wrapped trinket
safely inside her bag.

It was nearly five o'clock when she heard a
despairing female voice wail in an easy identifiable
transatlantic accent, 'It's no use, Ella May—this is the
street we've just come from. We're hopelessly lost!.'

It took a matter of seconds to retrace her steps and

locate the two middle-aged ladies to offer her assistance which was gratefully received.

'My dear, you've saved our lives,' the one who had been addressed as Ella May confided. 'Elvira here, my sister, felt we'd be able to see so much more if we went around by ourselves instead of being hustled about by a guide, but believe me, we've spent absolutely hours just trying to get out of this place!'

'And we still haven't seen the Kasbah, or the Sultan's Palace or the Treasury,' Elvira admitted sorrowfully. 'Oh, I could kick myself!'

Vida's sympathetic smile recognised her obvious distress. She wasn't in any hurry to return to the Villa—in fact the longer she stayed away the more effective her act of defiance would be. Besides, she'd had enough of male company.

'I could show you some of the tourist attractions,' she offered a trifle shyly. 'And probably some interesting things that aren't in the official guide books.'

'You live here?' Elvira's face mirrored her delight.

'I used to. Now—now I'm just revisiting.'

'Then we'd love you to, my dear!' Ella May responded warmly. 'Are you sure there's nothing else you ought to he doing?'

'Quite sure,' Vida told her firmly, experiencing the thrill of an errant schoolgirl playing truant. 'My time's entirely at my own disposal,' she added blithely.

It was half-past seven when exhausted but content, the two Americans declared themselves more than satisfied. 'Overjoyed!' Elvira announced. 'My dear Vida, you've saved our holiday. I declare we wouldn't have spoken a word to each other for months unless you'd come to our rescue.'

Seeing Ella May's grin, Vida knew the assertion to be untrue. They were charming people: warm, friendly and intelligent. She'd enjoyed herself greatly in their company and told them so, genuinely horrified when they tried to persuade her to accept a gift of money.

'Then have dinner with us,' begged Elvira. 'We're going back to our hotel this moment. Now, please, you can't refuse to share our table!'

'Unless, of course, you're expected elsewhere for dinner,' Ella May added, joining her entreating smile to that of her sister.

For the space of a second Vida hesitated, but she'd already burned her boats, hadn't she?

'No, I'm not expected anywhere,' she lied smoothly. 'I'd love to join you.'

The El Minzah was one of Tangier's most famous hotels and the food was a gourmet's delight. Her day in the open air, the relaxation of tension and most of all the company and conversation of the two delightful ladies had filled Vida with bonhomie.

Listening to the voluble talk of her companions as she made her way through hors d'oeuvre, main course and dessert, Vida did wonder what reaction she would get if she told them the truth about her enforced presence in Tangier. Probably they would be keen to help and would end up by making matters a great deal worse than they were already. Somehow, she knew, however the matter was finally resolved it had to be by Karim and herself alone.

She looked up from her plate, conscious suddenly that the prattle at the table had stopped. Both women were looking at her expectantly.

'I'm sorry?' she murmured apologetically.

'The man who was at the door, the one who's coming this way now . . . I just asked you if you knew him. The manager was with him, and he seemed to point out this table, and now he's coming across, so naturally I wondered . . .'?

Vida froze. It couldn't be! Karim wouldn't have even considered looking for her amid a city of half a million residents . . . let alone found her! Whoever it was would pass by their table and continue on his way . . .

She didn't turn, because she couldn't. Every muscle in her body seemed to have calcified. But she could tell by the interested expression on the raised faces of her new friends, the mixture of admiration and anticipation that shone in their eyes, that she was wrong, even before she felt his hand on her shoulder and heard his deep even-toned voice say gently, 'So here you are, Vida. Won't you introduce me to your friends?'

Of course he wouldn't drag her out by her hair in the middle of the El Minzah dining room, she told herself as she tried to conquer the erratic rhythm of her pulse. Karim wouldn't make a public exhibition of himself, he was too much the sophisticate for that. But he wanted to—she could feel it in every controlled breath he took, in the slightly spasmodic touch of his fingers on her shoulders, in the unnatural calm of his greeting. Karim was burning with volcanic fury!

She had known there would be a reckoning, of course she had. She had deliberately enticed it to satisfy her need for a declaration of independence. On the other hand, at the start of her expedition she had never meant to stay away for so long. An hour or two would have made her point. Some newly kindled spirit of bravado had driven her to extend the time, and meeting the American sisters had given her a false sense of security. Besides which it had made her lose track of the time. A glance at her watch showed it was ten-thirty.

Her bravery of the morning seemed much less significant now in the evening shadows, and the feeling of victory she had expected at arousing his temper was sadly lacking.

'I—I . . .' she stuttered awkwardly, then bowing to convention, painful though the words were to say, 'this is Karim—my husband.' She swallowed hardily. 'Karim, I'd like you to meet Elvira and Ella May from Arizona.'

'Husband?' echoed Ella May, extending her hand towards Karim. 'Why, Vida never told us she was married!'

'She tends to forget the fact sometimes,' he said tersely, returning the handshake end extending the same courtesy to Elvira.

'I'm afraid I shouldn't have stayed so long.' Hurriedly Vida rose to her feet. Any moment the sisters were going to invite Karim to join them, and an already volatile situation would go sky-high. 'Perhaps you'd both dine with us at our villa tomorrow,' she added impulsively. The thought of callers the following day might mitigate Karim's anger, she estimated hopefully.

'Oh, didn't we tell you, Vida dear?' It was Elvira who answered. 'We're leaving tomorrow on a coach tour to Agadir before we fly back to the States. But if you're ever in Arizona, you must both visit us.' She reached into her handbag, producing a visiting card. 'Here's our address.'

It was Karim, reaching over her shoulder, who

accepted it. 'Thank you,' he said courteously. 'I'm sure my wife will have every reason to remember meeting you.'

Vida shivered at the calmly spoken words, helplessly aware of the underlying threat behind his steady tone.

'She's a beautiful girl,' Ella May told him warmly. 'You wait till you hear what she did for us!'

'Believe me, it's a prospect I await with avid interest.' Vida started sharply as he lowered his head and touched her cheek just below the ear with gentle lips. 'And yes, she is indeed very beautiful, which is one of the reasons I'm sure you'll understand that I'm anxious to take her home after a whole day deprived of her company.'

Still neither of the Americans sensed the menace in his silky reply, Elvira blushing prettily at what she saw as a romantic implication, telling him fulsomely, 'You just make sure you take good care of her!'

'Of that, *madame*,' Karim said gravely, inclining his head in a typically French gesture of farewell, 'you may rest assured.'

Vida didn't speak on the journey back to the Villa. To *excuse* oneself, said the French proverb, was to *accuse* oneself, therefore silence was her best defence. She stared out of the window as the car covered the short distance.

Still not a word was uttered as Karim parked the car outside the small courtyard, assisted her from the passenger seat and marched her into her bedroom, pushing her with ungentle hands down on to the bed.

'Now, my lady,' he said, his voice trembling with a slow burning anger, his fine masculine body primed with an aggressive potency, 'you have ten seconds to tell me why I shouldn't beat you black and blue as a punishment for all the trouble you've caused!'

An involuntary gasp escaped her at the venom in his words as she made herself meet his smouldering gaze. Deep lines grooved his cheeks and she could see the tautness of his entire body reflected in the grim set of his jaw.

At the time the declaration of her independence and her courage to oppose him had seemed a worthwhile objective. It had been intended to put their relationship on a more realistic basis.

Perhaps, like the lemmings, she suffered from an inbuilt urge to orchestrate her own destruction? Because now, faced with Karim's pitiless appraisal, she felt decidedly less brave.

Resentment and rage came to her aid as a bitter tightness began to make her throat ache. Whatever happened she mustn't let herself be cowed by his ruthless brutality.

Resolutely ignoring the shiver of nervousness that coursed down her spine she glared back at him, a fierce pride making her blue eyes sparkle. 'I left you a note!'

Karim's eyebrows rose contemptuously over grimly intent eyes.

'Indeed you did,' he agreed. 'So you went shopping, Vida?' A small mocking pause. 'For thirteen hours?' He moved so quickly she had no time to intervene before he'd seized her bag, insolently tipping the contents out on to the bed beside her. 'How selective you must have been,' he mused as heat stained her cheeks at his impertinence. The sandals, poorly wrapped in the first place, tumbled out before his cool disdain.

'Don't touch it!' A sharp pain twisted inside her as he reached for the bracelet still securely hidden in its wrapping. She didn't want his connoisseur's eyes assessing the sentimental trinket to which she'd treated herself.

Karim didn't reply immediately, but he did replace the parcel, his mouth moving into the facsimile of a smile. 'Why? It was bought by my wife with my brother's money. Doesn't that give me a right to see your indulgences? Or is it perhaps a gift for a friend ... a lover?'

'Think what you like!' Nerves made her voice shake. 'What's the point of trying to explain anything to you? For a man with such an eye for artefacts, you're singularly blind where people are concerned!'

She sprang from the bed, too incensed to care what happened to her, and found her wrists grasped in a painful hold.

'Have you any idea of the chaos you've caused by your thoughtless behaviour?' His voice, deeply harsh, shook with a terrible fury, and a small sob escaped her as she felt his thumbs press agonisingly into her pulse points.

Jerking violently in his angry grasp, she dredged up every ounce of the hurt and resentment she had nurtured during the past year. 'Let me go!' she stormed.

'Not until you've listened to what I have to say to you.' Karim shook her once, hard, jerking her head back so that her pale hair whipped across her face. Too fighting mad to consider caution, Vida lashed out at him with her foot, yelling with shock and frustration as he forced his own leg between hers, taking her off balance and throwing her back on the bed. The words he spat out were in Arabic and would doubtless have made her cheeks burn if she'd been able to understand them.

He knelt across her body, controlling her flailing legs with his own weight, holding her arms in contact with the silken cover above her vainly-turning head. She could feel the violence in him, the muscular power of his legs, the bruising pressure of his hands, and she should have been terrified. Instead, with a sick sensation of shame she recognised the fire coursing through her veins as excitement and yes—humiliatingly, the precursor of desire.

Karim had nominally been her husband for a few short hours—but never her lover in the fullest sense of the word. He had bemused and charmed her, fêted her and adored her, promised so much of himself and given nothing!

Furiously Vida fought to control the tears of self-pity that threatened to overcome her. She had too much pride to cry in front of him. Whatever happened she wasn't going to beg for his mercy.

'You wanted to make me suffer!' The thickly lashed eyes accused her. 'Oh, yes, *mignonne*, I understood your motives, and at first they amused me.'

Amused? Yes, he certainly must have been amused if he really thought she had intended to make him suffer. She had never had illusions on that score. To make him annoyed—that was something quite different.

'When you didn't return for lunch, I told myself you were piqued because you were excluded from dining with my visitors yesterday.' He frowned. 'Women are like children at times, they imagine themselves insulted for no good reason and plan their petty revenges.'

Vida stayed silent with an effort. The goad was too obvious; she wouldn't be drawn by it.

'However, when you hadn't returned by five I had to take action, so I went to the police.'

Her eyes widened with genuine horror. 'The police? You went to the police because I went out shopping?' Embarrassment and horror made her squirm mentally as well as physically beneath his confining body. 'Oh, how could you! How demeaning!'

'Exactly.' Karim regarded her in the stretching silence, his coal-dark eyes grimly censorious. 'Especially when you were discovered happily dining hours later the best hotel in Tangier.'

'But how did they—I mean, I don't understand . . .' Her voice tailed away. She could feel Karim's body warmth reaching out to her, or was it she had turned abnormally cold? Not as cold as Karim's voice, though, as its icy tones supplied her with the information she had dreaded to ask.

'Fortunately, as you know, I have many friends in the local police. When I explained my concern for my wife who had recently returned to Tangier after an unavoidable absence and who had failed to return home after a shopping expedition they were very understanding and helpful. Eventually a young policeman reported seeing a woman of your description,' his hand left one shoulder to pick up a tress of flaxen hair before fingering the fabric of her dress as it lay taut against her breasts, 'in the company of two middle-aged American tourists. From there it was easy. The police register pinpointed the hotels where such visitors were staying, and discreet enquiries soon identified your friends. As soon as your whereabouts had been confirmed, I was told. The rest you know.'

He studied her face with a detached assessment she found as scary as his previous fury. 'It must give you a deep sense of satisfaction, imagining the laughter and ribald comments that are going on behind my back at this moment, hmm? Even friends will mock a man whose wife is so discourteous she publicly flouts his authority over her.'

Oddly enough Vida found no amusement in his being made fun of by his compatriots, but if that was what he wanted to believe—well, let him, she decided. He sighed, and the gleam in his eyes promised her no leniency as he asked gently, 'Just how many times do you think you can make a fool of me and get away with it unscathed, my beauty?'

'Why go to the police?' she demanded defensively. 'You knew there was nowhere I could go without money or a passport or friends. You knew I would have to come back.' Her face mutinous, she tried to roll away from him.

'Or be murdered, or robbed or raped!' Karim's breath rasped against her as he lowered his head to within inches of her face. 'Tangier can be as dangerous as London or New York, and if you had one grain of sense in your beautiful head you would have known the risks existed and that I couldn't disregard them.'

He was breathing in deep controlled breaths now as he stared into her expressive eyes. With a sick anticipation she recognised the flush of arousal on his lean cheeks for what it was.

'Why should it matter to me,' she flung back at him, 'whether I go out to the Medina and get raped or stay here and suffer the same fate!'

'Why indeed?' he agreed with ominous softness. 'But it matters very much to me, because I've waited too long already for this moment.'

There was no way she could escape the assault of his mouth as without either gentleness or patience it moved to possess her own. Automatically she resisted, pushing at his chest with the flat palms of her hands, her body arching upwards in useless defiance. Karim's mouth ravaged her until she stopped struggling and then with devastating suddenness he released her.

'Is that what you expected? What you wanted?' It had been intended as a punishment and it had hurt her deeply with its contempt. Vida closed her eyes, turning her head away from him, shamed to have invited his retribution and even more shamed because deep inside her a rebellious spiral of need and desire had started to spread a growing excitement to the core of her nervous system.

'Vida . . .' Karim groaned her name as if begging her reply, then when she refused to answer, he took her mouth again, this time with a heart-stopping tenderness that was infinitely more dangerous.

She knew she had moaned his name aloud as she responded mindlessly to the slow sweet seduction of her senses. Everything about him was intoxicating, from the soft warm nibbling caresses of his mouth to the delicate yet purposeful way he was moving his hands over her body, touching her as if she were something rare and precious. This was how it had been in the past. Her body knew and recognised it, melting towards his, offering itself up voluptuously, seeking the pleasures it had once known, eager to experience the untold pleasures his restrained passion had once promised her.

Time encapsulated as her own hands sought the exciting maleness of Karim's body, reaching to caress the smooth muscled expanse of his chest beneath the fine cotton shirt, tearing it open so she could rest her mouth on the warm damp skin, inhaling its scent, taking its flavour on her tongue. She wanted to take him into herself, to possess him, to take his pride, his passion, his stubbornness, the whole spirit that was Karim, and bind them together into one fearless eternal entity.

She was mesmerised, her body yielding and pliant as reluctantly he rose from the bed, pulling her with him. With trembling fingers he unbuttoned the front of her dress, pulling it away from her thrusting breasts, unfastening the simple bra she wore and cupping the pale heated flesh that quivered in his palms.

As his head lowered to enable his lips to pay a sensuous homage to their beauty, Vida held his dark head, twisting her fingers through his wealth of hair and making small inarticulate sounds of pleasure.

If he hadn't spoken, if he had simply seduced her with his touch, worshipped her with his silent mouth and subtle fingers, she would have played the game to the final score.

Afterwards, in the deep silence of the lonely night, she was to keep recalling the moment Karim overplayed his hand.

He gathered her against his ardent male body, its palpable excitement enticing her abandoned response. Gazing with fevered eyes into the limpidity of her answering regard, Karim spoke the words his intuition told him would be the final password to his goal.

'I love you,' he muttered. 'God knows how I love you!'

It was too false, too extreme, and it turned her blood to ice. Karim's final trump! A declaration of love to ensure her eager participation in an act of physical pleasure that would leave him triumphant and her demoralised and bereft.

Nothing had really altered. She was still his disgraced 'wife', to be possessed before being discarded, and he still had the utter nerve to demand her co-operation in her own mortification!

She would never, never make it that easy for him, although the cost to herself could be frighteningly high. She would not be used as his concubine!

'No more—that's enough!' Her fingers tightened on his head, trying to push him away.

He didn't believe her. His voice, throatily erotic, murmured against one tumid breast, 'I'll never have enough of you.'

'You'll never have me at all—willingly!' The sharpness of her voice pierced the throes of his sexual languor as effectively as a slap in the face. He raised his head, staring at her in disbelief—for all the world, she thought bitterly, like one of the Forty Thieves whose cave of treasures refused to open at the magic call of 'Open Sesame!'

'Vida?'

She hardened her heart against the husky plea, damping down the small panicky sensation that assailed her. She had to be adamant. No matter how much she wanted him to quench the fire she had allowed him to kindle inside her, to let him do so would lead to the total destruction of her self-esteem.

'I'm not your wife!' she blazed. 'I won't be used! I

won't let you ... let you...'

'Love you?' Karim's breathing was ragged as if every gasp was painful. She felt no pity, only an ever-increasing anger as the unsatisfied longings Karim's hands and mouth had awakened refused to subside.

'*Love's* not what you want!' she declared scathingly, feeling her stomach muscles tense as she met the stunning darkness of Karim's gaze with a haughty toss of her head. 'You've never made a secret of your opinion of me—a liar, a cheat, a whore ... a woman not fit to eat at the same table as your friends...' Despite her resolve her voice broke and she had to turn her face away abruptly, still held a prisoner by the power of his arms.

'By all that's holy!' The soft glow of the wall lights he'd switched on as they had entered the room cast shadows beneath his cheekbones, deepened the pools of his eyes, seemed to intensify the tautness of his mouth and the pallidity of his skin. 'You seem determined to misunderstand! The meeting was personal, confidential ... even my own brother was excluded!'

Vida fought down an insane desire to laugh. He'd totally ignored the more serious charges—because he had no answer to them.

'Vida, look at me.' His voice had softened, become cajoling. He mustn't see the effect he was having on her. Somehow she must hide the weakness of her legs, the painful constriction that threatened her breathing. She shut her eyes tightly, refusing to look at the face which could move her to fury one moment and stimulate an aching desire she was determined to resist, the next.

She felt his sigh shudder through his body. 'Is it

really impossible for you to believe that I still love you?'

His hands moved in leisurely caresses down her arms. She gritted her teeth to prevent the scream that would have released her feelings. Oh, how dared he torture her like this! He was more clever and unfeeling than she'd given him credit for; and the pain in her heart was so intense she felt it as a physical pressure.

The spasmodic movement of Karim's fingers stilled. His eyes dwelt on her face as she lifted her lids at last to obey his command, turning the full impact of her troubled gaze towards him.

It took every ounce of resolution bred by the past twelve months of loneliness and despair to oppose him, but she did.

'Yes, it's quite impossible.' She swallowed, her throat thick with an indeterminate pain. 'And after what's happened between us I resent your even pretending that you could.' His watchful expression invited her to continue. 'I realise I can't prevent you from doing whatever you wish to me, that there's no one here would come to my aid if I were to scream for help, but please, don't try to dignify what you have in mind by calling it love!'

Karim's breath hissed in as if she'd hit him. He started to speak then stopped as he saw the bright glitter of tears that had sprung to her eyes. For a moment he continued to stare at her defiantly challenging face, while she summoned up every effort of her will-power to prevent her tears falling. Then to her utmost relief he relinquished his hold on her.

'I see.' His eyes slid over her rigid form, making a thoughtful analysis. 'I must admit screaming is hardly the accompaniment I envisaged for 'what I had in mind", as you so eloquently describe it.' His voice was sardonic and there was little humour in the wry smile he bestowed on her. 'Perhaps after a good night's sleep you'll be in a different frame of mind tomorrow, *mignonne*.'

Without another word he moved away and left her too surprised to regret not having had the last word. She stayed rooted to the spot, listening to the outer door close and his footsteps dying away as he crossed the courtyard. Against all the odds, incredibly she had been reprieved.

Wearily she sank down on the soft bed. How many more days could she endure this torture? In the game that Karim was playing with her was his latest move meant to arouse her gratitude, or was it merely a way of drawing out her agony for his own amusement? Damn him for everything! Vida thought bitterly. For tormenting her mind and body, and most of all for leaving her here alone with nothing but a dreadful sense of anticlimax.

CHAPTER NINE

THAT night Vida slept uneasily, her dreams plagued with glamorous exciting memories from the past—dancing in an open-air night club, galloping along the sands, riding in a horse-drawn carriage round the walls of pink-ochre-built Marrakesh. And all the time her constant companion was Karim—laughing, talking, touching her, or just looking at her the way he used to before . . .

In the early hours of the morning she dreamed they became lovers, and awakened aching and unfulfilled because her imagination baulked at supplying what her experience lacked.

She dressed in a flared white skirt and cool navy cotton knit top. Her own fervid response to Karim had shaken her, leaving her uncertain of her own resolve. One enemy was bad enough, she hadn't thought she might have to fight herself as well. She shivered. God only knew how she would be feeling now if Karim hadn't made that one vital mistake. He was too experienced not to have known the extent of her own arousal. She supposed he wouldn't have gone away unless he'd been very sure of his eventual success. It was a conclusion that gave her no peace of mind at all.

He was standing by the side of the pool towelling himself down as she approached. Just the sight of his golden smoothly muscled body, so barely clad, was enough to make Vida catch her breath in admiration. Impotently she felt the warm colour rise to her face as

144

he looked up. Too conscious of the eroticism of her recent dreams, she glanced away.

'I've been waiting for you.' Karim flung his towel down on one of the chairs and followed it down, stretching long legs out before him and indicating that she sit opposite him. 'We have a lot to talk about.'

'I've said everything I have to say.' She shouldn't be here in Morocco in the first place, and she certainly wasn't going to explain or apologise for any of her actions, she determined darkly.

'In that case you can sit down and listen to me.' There was a formidable quality in the timbre of his voice that it would be foolish to ignore. Sullenly Vida did as bid, sparing one loaded look at his saturnine features before turning her attention to the food set out on the table between them.

Mentally she prepared herself for a lecture, even a list of sanctions which would be applied to her. She told herself stolidly she was prepared for everything!

'There's going to be a party here in the Villa tonight.'

Her head came up sharply at the drawled statement. Then she thought she saw his meaning.

'Really?' she countered lightly. 'I take it that means I shall be confined to my quarters again?'

'Hardly.' Eyes agleam with sardonic amusement met her cool appraisal. 'Since, *mignonne*, you are to be the guest of honour.' Then as her lips parted in genuine surprise, 'Don't look so shocked! It's quite natural for a husband to give a party to celebrate his wife's return to her rightful place.' Vida felt her whole body tremble beneath his raking scrutiny before he added with mocking gentleness. 'However short the duration of that return might be.'

'Oh, no!' This was too much. She wouldn't be publicly paraded. It was a fiendish plan and one that left a taste as bitter as gall in her mouth. 'Haven't you punished me enough already just by bringing me here?'

Karim's smile was little more than a twist of his beautiful mouth. 'It would be so unbearable for you?'

'What you intend would!' she cried desperately, her voice beginning to shake. 'How would the evening end? With a public divorce—is that what you have in mind?'

'No.' Karim's reply was low-key, but his eyes had narrowed speculatively. 'I thought you might enjoy it. My mother is coming up from Casablanca especially to meet you again, there will be about sixty other guests and I've arranged for an exhibition by the Guedra dancers. I recall you always wanted to see them perform.'

Vida met his faintly quizzical glance with rising agitation. Perhaps he wasn't about to engineer her public disgrace. If it was true that Khariya Gavigny had been invited it was unlikely he would embarrass his mother by such an action. Was she supposed to be impressed by his kindness, his generosity, his consideration? Good grief, he'd even remembered her expressed wish to see the Guedra! Was it his intention to offer her a sumptuous pleasure-filled trap now to bring her willingly to his bed? If so, she supposed she should be flattered by the persistence of his one-track mind. But it was still a trap, and she wouldn't be caught by his cold-blooded determination to treat her as a toy to be used, abused and thrown away.

'You can't *make* me go!' she flung at him, too disturbed to be cautious. 'I won't go, Karim. I won't pretend to be your wife!'

'Oh, I don't know. I think I can persuade you to come.'

The casual statement issued so silkily raised a shiver of apprehension. Her raised eyebrows invited his explanation.

'You, see I want very much for you to be at my side tonight. I want you there, radiant and beautiful as if it was the only place you had ever desired to be. I want you to be there as my wife until the last guest leaves.'

'And then?' Her throat seemed abnormally dry. 'What then, Karim?'

He was too powerful, too beautiful, too irresistible. The ambivalence of her own feelings was tearing her apart, she recognised with growing dismay.

'Then?' He gave a short laugh. 'Why, then, *mignonne*, you may claim your reward. You may go back to England.'

Before her astounded eyes, her passport appeared on the table, produced from Karim's carelessly abandoned clothes on a third chair.

To say she was stunned was to minimise the effect of his action. She was keenly aware of Karim's regard, the deep unfathomable stillness of his face, as the silence stretched between them.

'You mean to give it back to me after the party?' she asked uncertainly, sure there must be other conditions involved. Last night he had seemed so sure of himself, she could hardly believe she'd triumphed so easily.

'I'm giving it back to you now.' Karim pushed the blue pasteboard closer to her. 'Take it.'

She reached across, lifting the token of her release, and observing that her return ticket was also inside it.

'But but I could leave now, this morning!' she

protested wildly. 'I don't understand.'

His gaze slid over her and she felt herself hold her breath as the thoughtful scrutiny spared her nothing. At length, when she thought she could bear the quivering tension no longer, he said quietly, 'It's quite simple. I've changed my mind.'

'You'll really let me leave Tangier?' she asked shakily, totally unprepared for the painful tightness of her chest as his sharply analytical eyes assessed the depth of her reaction.

'If that's what you want.' Karim inclined his dark head affirmatively.

Of course it was! Vida's fingers tightened possessively on the passport as a movement in the cloisters foreshadowed the imminent arrival of Khalil. Could she believe him? Or could he summon up some Moroccan law which nullified the validity of the passport in her maiden name? Had Karim really revised his intentions, or was it one more move in the war of nerves he was waging against her?

'How do I know I can trust you?' she whispered.

'You don't,' he agreed quietly. 'Any more than I can trust you to play the part I ask of you for one more day. Shall we say it's an exchange of mutual trust, *mignonne*?'

Wordlessly Vida returned his level gaze, still uncertain of the motive behind his volte-face. His voice softened, deepened. 'I can't enforce your presence tonight, but I do entreat it.'

What harm could her agreement do? She knew she was weakening, hated the flaw in herself that couldn't hold out against the charm and charisma that emanated from the lean body and personable face of the man who held her gaze so avidly.

Probably, she thought wearily, Karim had already discovered there was no flight available to London before the next day anyway. He must have arranged the party days if not weeks before her arrival, if he'd hired dancers and invited Khariya. Her thoughts tumbled restively even while she knew that every moment of hesitation was sapping her strength to say 'no'.

He must be asking her co-operation to save difficult explanations, she surmised. After yesterday's escapade her presence in the city wouldn't be unknown to many of Karim's friends. She supposed her absence would cause comment and shame him, though heaven only knew how he would explain her leaving the country again so shortly afterwards. But she'd won, hadn't she? She had finally persuaded him that she wanted nothing from him and could give him nothing in return, certainly not the total subjugation he had demanded. In victory she could afford to be generous.

'If that's all you want, then yes, I agree. I'll be there tonight,' she said at last, keeping her manner coolly detached despite the gathering pace of her heartbeat as she watched a slow smile of satisfaction soften the hard lines of his handsome face.

'It will do for a start,' he said ambiguously, rising to his feet and gathering up his abandoned shirt and trousers, before lifting a lazy hand of greeting towards Khalil as his brother approached. 'And now, if you'll forgive me, *mignonne*, there is much I must do.'

That evening Vida contemplated her appearance with a quiet satisfaction as she stood before the long mirror that fronted the fitted wardrobes in her room. She had never thought of red as being her colour. Like many blondes she had dressed in soft blues and turquoises to enhance the colour of her eyes. The ruby velvet evening dress had been Karim's choice in the happier days when he had gone shopping with her in the exclusive shops of the Boulevard Pasteur for her trousseau. She had never worn it apart from the few moments when she had tried it on. Now she surveyed it with detachment. Complete with its own silk cami-knickers, tailored to skim yet support the slim but voluptuous curves of her young body, the dress was a masterpiece from its neckline which dipped to show the promising cleavage between her breasts, to the cross-cut skirt which swayed and caressed her long shapely legs with every movement.

There was no vanity in admitting she had never looked better; the dramatic colour of the dress provided a striking foil to her fairness and seemed to add an extra sparkle to her long-lashed eyes. It had been a strange day altogether, she mused, her fingers plucking at the velvet enjoying the soft luxurious texture. The Villa had been swarming with caterers and electricians. A small pavilion had been erected behind the swimming pool for the use of the dancers, lights had been suspended from the trees, folding doors pushed back and furniture rearranged, giving the Villa a look like something out of the Arabian Nights.

Left to her own devices, Vida had spent the morning swimming and sunbathing beside the pool.

Karim's mother had arrived in the early afternoon and the four of them had shared a light lunch on the terrace before Khariya Gavigny, complaining of feeling tired after the long drive up from Casa, had retired to her room.

To be honest, Vida had been pleased to see her go. She had been dreading the meeting with the older woman, and certainly Khariya had done nothing to make the confrontation easier. She had been polite and distant, confining her attention to her two sons and including Vida in the conversation only when courtesy demanded it.

Not that Vida blamed her. She had met Khariya only once previously—on the day she had married her elder son. Whether she'd been taken into her son's confidence or not, there had been no way Khariya could have regarded her absent daughter-in-law with anything but contempt.

Vida's fingers touched her hair lightly as she half-turned to regard her own profile. Having nothing better to do she had spent a great deal of time copying a style a hairdresser friend had once demonstrated. The end result was a golden coronet constructed from her own hair, encircling the crown of her head. The remaining hair, thick and lustrous, fell smoothly to her shoulders.

Karim would be pleased with her appearance, she thought with a thrill of pleasure—and wondered immediately why his approbation should suddenly mean so much to her.

'Well!'

Vida spun round towards the door as a soft, feminine voice punctured her reverie. 'So now the falcon flies again you return to offer him your delicate wrist to perch on!'

The sudden appearance of Khariya startled her so much it was seconds before she could divine the meaning of the remark, spoken in Parisian French. When she did she found it hard to bite back a smile.

Karim in the role of a desert falcon seemed a very apt description. But she, Vida, as his mistress? No, rather her role was that of a small bird pursued and broken by his superior power. It was a fact she would never convince Karim's mother of, and she wasn't sure she even meant to try.

'Won't you come in and sit down?' she asked politely.

'Thank you. I did knock, but you must have been too engrossed with your preparations to have heard me.' Darkly analytical eyes swept her from head to foot, before Khariya Gavigny emitted a long deep sigh. 'Seeing you again makes it easier to understand my son's obsession with you. Yours is a cool, pure beauty which projects a sense of the unobtainable which is so obviously lacking in most other women of your race.'

There was no compliment in the remark, no warmth in the beautifully modulated voice. Whatever Khariya had come to say, it was obviously not to offer the hand of friendship or family!

Vida regarded her calm, oval face with resignation. In her early fifties, Karim's mother still possessed a stunning loveliness; her black hair showed no sign of grey, her olive skin was smooth, her mouth full and firm, her figure beneath the royal blue silk dress she wore was as slim and curvaceous as that of a woman twenty years her junior. In features her face more closely resembled her younger son's, with none of the sharply sculpted bones that made Karim's appearance so striking. The only hardness on Khariya's face was in the depth of her penetrating regard.

'Why have you returned to my son?' the slightest pause, then the courtesy title spoken with a cool impertinence—'*madame*?'

'Karim sent Khalil to England to fetch me,' Vida answered honestly. She and this woman were virtually strangers. It was impossible to confide in her, yet the last thing Vida wanted was to offend her.

'So when you learned that your husband was well and whole again you rediscovered your affection for him?' Elegantly defined eyebrows flared questioningly.

'It wasn't quite like that . . .' Vida demurred, uncertain how to cope with the flow of animosity aimed at her.

Khariya gave a brief laugh. 'I'm hardly surprised! Tell me, what kind of woman is it who turns her back on the man she married when he lies crippled, perhaps dying?'

Dear God, this was going to be even worse than she'd feared! Hostility lay like a cold mist between them, and Vida had no idea how to even begin to dispel it. At last she said tentatively, 'I don't know how much you know . . .'

Khariya shrugged expressive shoulders.

'I know Karim married you. I know you left him— some argument over the man who nearly killed him, I believe. I know, too, that when my son was near death and afterwards when for several weeks he wished he *had* died, you didn't come to him.'

Desperately Vida fought down the sense of shame that engulfed her. 'I had no idea what had happened . . .'

'There are no phones in England? No way a wife having deserted her husband, can communicate with him?' Bitterness coloured each question. 'I only know it was *my* hand he gripped when the pain became unendurable, and *my* fingers that wiped the sweat from his forehead, and it was *my* cheek that rested against his when in his delirium he called your name again and again . . .'

Vida held back tears of sudden anguish with an effort. 'We'd quarrelled,' she said in a low voice. 'He was so angry I—I was terrified of what he might do.'

It seemed a weak excuse without the threat of his actual words and the background against which they had been hurled at her, and she wasn't surprised when the other woman looked at her in disbelief.

'*Tiens!* And what did you think my son would do to you? Did you think he might thrash you? And what if he had? How much would he have hurt you before his anger turned to desire and he became your slave instead of your master?' Khariya gave a scornful laugh. 'Were you so unsure of yourself that you couldn't use your charms to turn his anger to love? Or had you betrayed him so badly you dared not beg his mercy?'

'He thought I had!'

It was a cry from the heart as Vida faced the arrogant appraisal of the jeering brunette. 'But he was mistaken!' Her voice broke. 'There was no way I could explain the truth,' she continued desperately. 'I couldn't face his anger—I was terrified! Surely you can understand that?' Her eyes pleaded with unknowing pain darkening their colour.

'No.' Khariya's face was as cold as her voice. 'If you had loved him you would have suffered anything at his hand rather than turn your back on him!' She made an impatient gesture with her hand as Vida struggled to find words of self-justification. 'Let me speak frankly to you.'

For the first time since entering the room she seated herself in one of the armchairs, waving Vida imperiously towards the other. 'I have loved two men in my life, and I bore each one of them a son. My father was a merchant—dealing in gold and gems— and I was with him in the Emirate of Al-Khazar-ja when I first saw Ahmar—Karim's father. I was just seventeen and he was three years older. Love at first sight,' her shoulders moved eloquently, 'call it what you will. He was the most beautiful man I had ever seen, and my awareness of it must have shone from my eyes as he looked at me—and oh, how he looked!' Khariya paused as the joy of her memories warmed her expression.

'He was the Emir's second son, and as was customary a marriage had long since been arranged for him. But he won his mother to our side and she was a powerful ally. Eventually the Emir agreed to our wedding.'

This time the pause was long, while Vida sat silent, entranced by the beauty on the face of her companion. 'Karim was conceived in joy and passion, wildly and gloriously, on a silk-covered couch in a room darkly lit with silk-shrouded hanging lamps, with the Oriental wrought-iron grilles throwing their shadows across the mosaic tiling of the floor, while the stars glowed white in the black sky of a cold desert night!'

Before the glowing descriptive words, Vida bowed her head, moved by Khariya's passion, feeling an answering throb of emotion bridging the gap between them. Khariya stared down at her own slender fingers, her voice sunk to a whisper. 'Ahmar was an idealist, full of enthusiasm and purpose. He wanted to use his family's power to do wonderful things for his small country. He was a natural leader. His elder brother was his father's heir, but it was Ahmar the tribesmen loved. In personality and appearance he had no peer.'

Again the quality of her voice changed, becoming strained. 'He was twenty-five years of age when he was shot dead by an assassin's bullet and left to die alone in the desert.'

'I'm so sorry...' Vida breathed her regrets, knowing the words were inadequate, but unable to stay silent before the sadness of Khariya's expression.

But it seemed as if the Moroccan woman hadn't heard her interjection as she continued evenly, 'After his death, the Emir wanted me to join his family with Karim. But Ahmar had given me total freedom. I couldn't face the close supervision I would have had as part of the Emir's family. There was a French journalist—Charles Gavigny—whom Ahmar had known. He was many years older than I and unmarried because his job took him away from his Paris home so much, but it was to him I turned for help in those black days. It wasn't easy, but in time he found a way out for me and Karim. He took us back to France and he and I were married.'

She sighed deeply, leaning back in the chair and closing her eyes. 'Khalil was conceived six years later, in gratitude and affection, gently and happily, in the warm bed of a Paris flat when the soft rain washed the opening candles of the chestnut trees by the Tuileries Gardens.'

Her dark eyes opened abruptly as she leaned forward, fixing Vida with an unwavering gaze. 'When Charles died of a heart attack four years ago, Karim was already running a successful business here in Morocco. There was nothing left for me in Paris, and as Khalil was eager to discover for himself the other side of his heritage we came here also. Now, when I look at Karim, it is as if his father were alive again—the resemblance is so strong. Ahmar was murdered before he had even reached Karim's age, yet when I look at my son I see my husband as he would have been!'

She rose suddenly, but not before Vida had seen the welling tears; but there was no trace of them as she turned fiercely. 'Love has more than one face, *madame*, as my own history relates, but I would not be the woman I am if I didn't want for Ahmar's son what he and I shared for so brief a time.' The torrent of words ceased as Khariya paused, letting her blazing eyes sweep over the pale face of the young woman in front of her.

'Are you the woman who can give him that kind of devotion?' she demanded peremptorily. 'And if you are, why have you confined yourself to these apartment like some concubine? What have you come back for, *belle-fille*? What do you want from my son—payment to dissolve this strange alliance, or the pleasure of manipulating his future once more?'

'Madame ... please ...' Vida protested, shocked and disturbed by the spirited attack.

'Hm!' Khariya made a sound of muted disgust. 'You're astonished I should speak to you in this manner. Learn now that the bonds of family life in Islam are deep and strong and nowhere in the world will you find a more lasting affinity between mother and son. It must be on my conscience for life that I cheated Karim of his father's name. I will not stand silent and see him cheated again, as you will learn to your cost!'

Too upset by Khariya's obvious sincerity and the touching depth of feeling she had expressed for Karim to be angered by her threat, Vida bent her head forward into her hands, fighting the faintness that threatened her.

'I'm sorry,' she gasped. 'There's nothing I can say to you, except that I'm powerless to influence Karim one way or the other. If you want an answer to your questions you must ask *him* why I'm here, what he feels about me.'

She was shaking now, giving a little cry as Khariya rose, coming towards her and forcing her chin upright so she could gaze down into her white face.

'I *know* what my son feels for you. A year ago he could have returned to Al-Khazar-ja as a leader of men. In the turmoil of progress the tribesmen of the Fahadazeen were looking for a new leader to take them to political power. Who better than Karim ibn Ahmar? The son of a father who had become a legend? Wealth, power, the adulation of men . . .' There was pride and pain on the olive-skinned face that transfixed Vida with its passion. 'And he turned it all down because he loved a little European girl more than anyone or anything else, and in the world he was being offered there would be no place for her.'

The cool fingers released their pressure. The delicate fragrance of expensive perfume grew fainter as Khariya stood away. 'That, Madame Belle-fille,' she declared haughtily, 'was the extent of my son's love for you.'

CHAPTER TEN

'I HAD no idea . . .' Vida swallowed convulsively, her mind spinning with the import of this new intelligence. So much of Karim's private life had been a secret from her. It was something she had hoped to change as their love had matured with marriage. She moved her head despairingly, 'No wonder you dislike me so much! If it hadn't been for me . . .'

'You mistake my meaning,' Khariya interrupted abruptly. 'I am selfish enough to be grateful to you that Karim chose not to enter so dangerous and cruel an arena. Al-Khazar-ja robbed me of a dearly loved husband. You think I would want to sacrifice a son to its demands as well? No.' She walked towards the door, turning at the threshold. 'If I dislike you, it is because I believe you are not woman enough for a man like Karim. It seems to me your outer beauty hides a spirit that lacks loyalty and stamina.' Standing, one hand poised on the door, dignified and lovely, she delivered her *coup de grâce*. 'If I have misjudged you, then you will forgive me, because we share a common love. If I am right, then you will do well to take whatever settlement Karim is prepared to make on you and get out of his life before you bring disaster down on your own lovely head!'

Twenty minutes later, when in response to her faint invitation to enter, Karim himself walked into the room, Vida was still sitting where Khariya had left her, feeling as if she had been caught in a whirlwind, totally unable to make sense from her turbulent thoughts.

'I began to think you might have changed your mind.'

Her breath caught in her throat as she rose unsteadily to her feet. Dressed in black trousers and a light tuxedo, Karim looked every inch the desert prince his antecedence proclaimed him. Formal and polite, he awaited her answer, only the intense darkness of his eyes betraying his concern.

'I'm just a little nervous.' The way Vida's voice trembled seemed to confirm her explanation, as his eyes travelled in purely masculine approval over the picture she presented.

'Every other woman here tonight will pale beside you,' he told her softly. His hands cupped her face as he added musingly, 'A lily and a rose ... Tonight, *mignonne*, like Gilbran's lady, you take your beauty to the fair for all men to see, and each one will desire you.'

'No,' she riposted quickly, denying it, strangely moved by the sadness of the smile he turned on her, 'they wouldn't dare. They will believe I belong to you.'

The look Karim gave her was long and hard, then without a word he felt in his pocket, opening out his hand to her. On his palm lay her wedding ring and the ruby and diamond cluster she had left behind the evening she had left him.

'Wear them tonight.'

It was an order, not a request. She had gone too far down this path already to quibble at this further requirement. Too shaken by her violent confrontation with Khariya, she let him take her hand, seeing from the glimmer of a smile on his mouth that her compliance pleased him, and allowed him to slide the rings over her finger.

'And this as well.' He produced a slim leather jeweller's box, and placed it in her hands.

Intrigued, she opened it, turning amazed eyes towards him as she realised the value of the gold necklet set with rubies that lay within. This time it was impossible to obey him.

'I can't take anything like this from you.' She had wanted kindness, understanding and above all trust— qualities of inestimable value but obviously beyond the gift of the man who still called her wife.

Karim ignored her protest; taking the necklet from its box, he moved behind her to fasten it round her neck. It lay, a scintillating collar on her creamy skin.

'Indulge me, Vida,' he said softly as her hands rose to her throat. 'I bought it for you on our wedding day. You know the customs of Islam. When a man is pleased with his woman he buys her gold.' She watched transfixed as pain darkened his pupils. 'I was going to give it to you the next morning—instead . . .'

Instead they had been apart—he in hospital, she in England. It had to be a cruel joke he was perpetrating on her, a cynical offering to belittle her. Were there no limits to what she would be asked to endure tonight?

'Then, as you are well aware, it's even more impossible for me to wear it!' Her hands rose in agitation, vainly trying to find the catch.

'Stop!' Her fingers dropped nervelessly as she stood in hostile silence before the potency of the single barked word. Agonisingly her lips began to tremble before the dark hauteur of his gaze. 'There's no price tag attached to it. Accept it as a parting gift, if you like—a token of regret for all the inconvenience I have caused you. Wear it with pleasure—you won't be asked to pay for it!'

'Karim—please . . .' God knew what she was begging for. But the dreadful emptiness inside her forced his name from her lips.

'Courage, petite femme!' His smile was faint, but at least it drained the irritation from his face. Before she realised his intention he had lowered his head and kissed her briefly full on her soft mouth. 'Your ordeal is nearly ended. Come, our guests will be arriving.'

Since there was no rational option Vida took his proferred hand, filled with an indescribable sadness as his strong fingers laced through her own, and allowed him to lead her towards the stage where she would play out her charade as she had promised.

Sipping a glass of Montrachet, Vida stood back in the shadows watching the beautifully gowned and dressed guests enjoying themselves. Greeting Karim's friends hadn't been the ordeal she had feared. Without exception they had treated her courteously with open pleasure, and if they had been surprised at her sudden reappearance they had been at great pains to disguise the fact.

They seemed to come from many walks of life, she observed to herself, enjoying the refreshing coolness of the wine while her gaze wandered over the groups of people, espying Khariya in animated conversation with a man she remembered as being the director of an international bank.

Of Karim there was no sign. She experienced a feeling of unease at his disappearance. It must be nearly an hour since she had last been in his company, dancing with him, her breasts hard against his chest, his strong thighs guiding her with masterly ease to the rhythm of the music. He had created a fantasy setting for her and for those few brief moments she had relaxed and allowed herself to enjoy it.

Closing her eyes, she had pretended the bitter abyss between them had never opened. It had been a mistake. Coming back to reality as the music ended, she had smiled mistily up into Karim's face, to find herself painfully snubbed by the grimness of his expression. At least she must be grateful he was letting her leave without fulfilling his threats, although she suspected wistfully that his change of mind had pivoted on the integrity of his own nature rather than on anything she herself had said or done. Despite everything Karim remained a man of honour. That alone earned him her respect.

A roll of drums shattered her musings, bringing her sharply back to the present. Midnight! The hour of the Guedra. Ever since she had come to Morocco Vida had longed to see a genuine performance of the dance that had originated under the nomad tents in the love courts of the Tuareg warriors. All she knew about it was that because the tents were so low, the dancers were unable to stand upright, so they had to kneel and all the 'dancing' was done with the upper part of their bodies.

Like all folk dances, many of the exhibitions put on for tourists were sub-standard and not worth watching. Tonight would be different, she knew, for Karim had arranged for the foremost dancers in Morocco to be their guests.

Determined not to miss the show, she lifted her long skirt slightly and followed the crowd towards the raised area beyond the pool from where she could look down on the circular part that had been turned into an impromptu stage.

Suddenly all the lights went out and the hum of voices stopped. Now there was an air of expectancy among the watchers as the performance area filled with dark hooded figures. Four large braziers had been lit and glowed redly in the darkness. Above the stars were bright, but there was no moon. As her eyes grew accustomed to the reduced light Vida saw a group of men carrying long torches approach the braziers, dip them into the flames and transport them glimmering and flickering.

It was then the drumming began—a steady monotonous beat that heightened the senses, promising excitement and drama. A sudden movement signified the expansion of the circle of drummers and as her eyes pierced the glow of the fires, Vida could see that in the centre of the ring, entirely covered by a black veil, lay a woman.

The drumbeat changed. The air of expectancy deepened and from beneath the veil the woman's hands emerged, white fluttering birds that dipped and dived, reached and pleaded, each subtle finger movement compelling in its sensuality.

Tension thrummed through the watching crowd as the men surrounding the girl started making ecstatic noises, humming, crying, wailing in a way that caught at Vida's throat.

There was a movement behind her, a lean hand on her arm, the fingers dipping down to catch her wrist. Karim's grasp tightened possessively on her bare flesh and she felt him tremble. Pinioned by the drama unfolding before her, she couldn't turn and look at him, but she made no effort to avoid the close contact of his body.

The rising beat of the drums now became augmented by a rhythmic hand-clapping which balanced and complemented the soft moaning voices. The girl's hands plucked desperately at the air, drawing and begging, her whole upper body beneath the flimsy veil moving in undulating, erotic time to the drumbeat and hand-clapping.

The spectators were silent, watching entranced. Suddenly a man stepped forward and plucked the black veil away from the girl. She was revealed moving from left to right hypnotically as if in a trance, her eyes closed, her face turned upwards. In the torchlight her breasts gleamed naked, proudly tumescent. The chanting grew more wild, the dancer's movements more voluptuous as the drumbeat quickened.

Karim had loosed Vida's wrists to enclasp her waist, drawing her even closer to himself. Subconsciously she had crossed her own arms, reaching out to accept and intensify his embrace, her fingers tightening on his arms as the tempo quickened.

The metamorphosis happened in a heartbeat. One moment Vida was watching, the next it was as if her spirit had entered the body of the Tuareg girl and it was she who was kneeling to welcome her warrior lover back to his desert camp. She could feel the girl's ecstasy coursing in her own body, know her desire, the hunger for the love of a brave strong man that would be wild and glorious and unrestrained! As the rhythm built inexorably to its brainstorming climax Vida went with it, totally committed to its message. She *was* that girl, warm and supple, aching for love, offering herself without qualification to her lover. To Karim.

Pleasure, pain, excitement and passion—it was all there, and the crowd sighed with a collective breath as the rhythm reached its unbearable climax—and stopped. And the dancer collapsed where she knelt, unconscious.

A group of men moved forward, gently lifted the supine figure and carried her away. From the performers' pavilion another girl under a similar black veil was carried in to the arena. The dance was beginning again.

At last Vida knew the truth. It was as if the removal of the veil from the Guedra dancer had stripped away the veil from her own emotions. Whatever logical reasons she had devised as an excuse to return to Morocco, there had been one overriding explanation. She had come back because she still loved Karim, had never stopped loving him. Before the power of the feeling she acknowledged for him there was no room for self-pride. No longer could she make conditions. Of course she still wanted his trust and understanding, but she couldn't demand them.

In those last few moments Karim's physical desire for her had been unmistakable. Demanding and possessive, his body had kept no secret from her and she had exulted to feel the trembling tension that racked his frame.

He still wanted her! And with her newly discovered self-revelation she would deny him nothing. There was never going to be a sure way she could prove she hadn't betrayed him, but there was a chance he would realise that by her total unconditional surrender to him she was demonstrating the absoluteness of her love, and even if he didn't, she knew she had no choice.

In the instant she was turning towards him, her love for him lending her face an ethereal beauty, Karim muttered something unintelligible, forcing his eyes away from the open pleading of her wide-pupilled eyes. Then to her horror he was moving away, leaving her standing alone.

If she had one remnant of pride left she would have stayed where she was, but it was an attribute she had already abandoned. Karim had wanted to make love to her! She knew it! Yet it was equally obvious he had no intention of attempting to do so with or without her consent. At the moment she had realised the depth of her love for him, ached to welcome him back to her heart and her body, he was denying her the opportunity.

It was her own fault. Yesterday she had taunted him with attempted rape, told him she would never go to him willingly, spiritedly denied the validity of their marriage contract. It was what she had wanted, this total alienation—or what she had thought she wanted. But love had neither logic nor pride. She only knew she must go to him.

Murmuring her excuses, she pushed her way through the rapt audience, stumbling a little in her high-heeled sandals, her long skirt hampering her from reaching him before he disappeared inside the Villa.

Following him, Vida stepped over the threshold. The place was deserted; everyone drawn to the spectacle taking place outside. Her breath coming in deep sobs, she followed the sound of Karim's footsteps as they ascended the staircase, knowing instinctively

he would he making for the master suite. Trembling at
her own boldness but too far committed to draw back
now her decision was made, she pushed open the door,
entering without knocking.

At the far side of the double bed, with only the light
of a bedside lamp to guide him, Karim was tearing off
his formal clothes with a vicious abandon. The tuxedo
lay roughly discarded over the back of a chair as his
lean fingers snatched at the buttons of his pleated
evening shirt. Thrown on the bed were dark cotton
cords and a casual shirt.

'Oh, dear heaven!' Her hands flew to her throat.
'What are you doing? Where are you going?'

'Go back to the Guedra, Vida. Leave me alone.' He
didn't even raise his eyes to her horror-stricken face as
the last button on the expensive shirt ripped off,
spinning across the mosaic-tiled floor, and he
wrenched the damaged garment from his back with
urgent fingers.

'So you can go to—to your mistress?' she challenged
totally without discretion, her face white above the
glinting gold of the collar he had placed round her
neck. He was burning with an unquenchable fire, and
her wild surmise had sprung from the only explanation
she could think of. Jealousy was a searing pain at the
thought that he meant to take any woman other than
herself to his bed.

'Mistress?' He gave a short bitter laugh, standing
with the shirt dangling from his hand, raising dark
fathomless eyes to regard her for the first time, as she
recoiled from the grim tortured expression with which
he confronted her. 'Even if such a person existed, I'd
take her no joy tonight!'

'Then don't go! Don't leave me!' She moved round

the bed towards him, hands extended in supplication.

'Don't try to stop me . . .' There was roughness in his voice as he reached to rid himself of the immaculate evening dress trousers.

'No!' Vida defied him, uncaring, her eyes blazing, furious that she couldn't find the words she needed to reach him. 'You can't go out like this . . .'

'I can do whatever I wish.' The lines of strain were showing white round his mouth, making it impossible to forgo the thought that he might actually strike her. 'Can't you see I don't want you here?'

Vida gasped painfully at the angry denial as every instinct told her it was a lie. Karim didn't love her, but he did want her. Even if she could explain how she felt there was no time for words. His self-control was stretched as tight as a guitar string.

'You don't understand,' she faltered, her mouth dry with the enormity of what she was daring. 'Tonight everyone believed I was your woman . . . your wife. I want to believe it too.' Please God, don't let her lose her courage now! 'I want you to make me believe it.' Despite her resolve her voice shook and she had difficulty in keeping her eyes fixed on him.

His face deathly pale, his eyes luminous and shadowed, Karim met her unwavering glance. She watched the hard painful movement of his larynx as he seemed to fight for words. 'Are you really set to destroy us both?'

Destroy? Dear God, he had undreamed of depths of cruelty. Wasn't she offering him what he had contemptuously told her was his right? How could he flail her so harshly with his words? Yesterday she hadn't been untouchable. What further sin had she

committed in his eyes to lower her even more in his
esteem?

'To love me would destroy you?' She flung back her
beautiful head, the golden crown of hair giving her the
appearance of some nineteenth-century Madonna.

'You think I'm callous?' He had read so well the
anguish on her face. 'Believe me, tonight isn't the time
to prove you wrong!' Turning and moving away from
her, Karim divested himself of the formal trousers and
reached towards the bed for the cords.

How much further must she humble herself in
expiation of the sins he had burdened her with? Must
she crawl to him defenceless and naked on her
stomach in total submission before this scion of a
desert prince would forgive her enough to take her into
his arms and give her the arrogant consolation of his
body?

'Wait!' Her tone was peremptory. There was no
humility in love freely given, passion freely shared and
enjoyed.

Surprised, he hesitated, as her fingers rose to the zip
at the back of her dress, closing as well on the lingerie
zip that secured the delicate undergarment. Her eyes
blazing with indomitable purpose into his entranced
face, Vida lowered both.

The dress still held her shape as she continued
speaking in an even tone. 'The night you asked me to
marry you, you told me you wanted me to stand before
you wearing only your gifts.' She took a deep breath,
scared yet exhilarated by what she knew she had to do.
Kicking off her shoes, she shrugged away the dress
and the flimsy garments beneath it, stepping away
from the pile of ruby velvet in one smooth movement.
Standing before him, naked and beautiful, fighting

the temptation to cover with her hands what no man had ever looked upon with love, she tried to tell him she loved him, but her throat closed convulsively, burying the words. Her eyes bright with her own temerity, she could only stare at his beloved face.

For one awful, soul-shattering moment she thought Karim meant to reject her, had perhaps intended all along to make her humble herself in supplication before him and then spurn her. This perhaps had been his revenge and she had played right into his hands. *Mektoub*, she thought, standing still as a statue. It has been written thus.

Then Karim moved, came towards her, lifting her in his arms, burying his head against the warm voluptuousness of her breasts.

'Oh God, have mercy on me—on both of us!' The words came brokenly from his lips as he laid her gently on the bed, pausing only to strip away the dark briefs that were the last remaining barrier between their mutually seeking bodies.

As flesh touched quivering flesh, Vida accepted Karim unrestrainedly into her arms, curling up beneath him, offering herself explicitly to his over-whelming need, welcoming him in total consummation of the love she had for him.

She cried out his name as he claimed her, heard her own name torn from his mouth in an agonising gasp and abandoned her mind and her body to his pleasure. It was over in seconds, total, complete, as sudden as the final orgasmic climax of the Guedra dance. As satisfying and as shattering.

CHAPTER ELEVEN

THERE were were no words to describe how Vida felt. She had taken Karim to herself, rejoiced in accepting the seeds of his manhood, absorbed his warmth and his strength, becoming truly one with him for a sparkling interval of time. The experience had enriched her life and would remain with her for always.

It didn't matter that he had ceased to love her, had already dismissed her from his home and his country because her own love in the breathtaking moment of climax had been bountiful enough to enshrine them both. Karim was, until he chose to speak the words of separation, still her husband in the only place that mattered—her heart. Now she had no wish to deny it. She had given him service and respect this night and with her body still filled with his sweetness she felt no shame—only pride in her total surrender.

Stirring, she cast shadowed eyes towards where Karim had moved, a little away from her, his face buried in the pillow, his hands clenched at the side of his head, knuckles showing white. Her eyes traced the long line of his naked back, lingering on the scars that shone white against the tanned skin. A spasm of pain tightened her tender mouth as she suffered vicariously for his past agony.

Impulsively she lowered her head, seeking the damaged tissues with her lips, trailing their moist softness down the length of the surgeon's incision,

moving them gently on the satin skin to nuzzle the
distorted bone.

It was only when she felt a deep shudder tremble
through him that she gave a little cry and withdrew her
mouth, every nerve in her body reacting to his
repulsion.

He still despised her, she thought forlornly, unable
to stop a sobbing breath escape in her despair. Now
she could see it had been his abiding distaste for what
he still saw her as that had prevented him from
claiming her as his wife as he had threatened, and not
her own opposition.

She had been mad to dream otherwise. Her throat
tight with unshed tears, Vida swung her legs off the
bed. She had to get out of here, leave Karim before he
spoke the words of recrimination and loathing that
must be hovering on his tongue.

'Wait!'

All the dark bitterness she had expected was in that
one word, as she tried vainly to elude the long arm that
reached out to restrain her. 'What do you want me to
say?' Karim's tone roughened as he pulled himself
upright to turn his dull-eyed gaze on her pleading face.
'I tried to warn you. You should have let me go while I
still had the strength to leave you. Why didn't you,
Vida . . . why?'

Why indeed? she thought wretchedly. Certainly not
so there could be a post-mortem on her emotions
afterwards. If he didn't realise she loved him there
were no words to convince him. Still the insistent
grasp on her arm demanded an answer.

'I don't know what to say to you,' she stumbled out
miserably at last.

'You could start by telling me I'm as brutal and

savage as you always thought I'd be. That I took you like an animal takes its mate, without affection or consideration!' The pain was raw in his voice, confounding her. 'Tell me, Vida,' he persisted hoarsely. 'Let me hear the names I deserve to hear. Call me what you will, lash me with your tongue for what I've done to you this night—anything—but don't leave me like this!'

Gradually a glimmer of his meaning penetrated her dulled senses. Still bemused by his anguished plea, she let her head drop down to his shoulder, resting her cheek against the polished skin above the taut muscles. What did a woman say to reassure the man she loved in such circumstances? A small sigh escaped her. The truth, of course.

'What names should I call you, Karim?' she said softly. 'Honest, powerful, needful . . .'

'Oh, yes, all those,' he agreed in a low voice fraught with anguish. 'And they leave me shamed and humiliated by my inadequacy!'

'Inadequacy?' Vida's mind reeled from his self-castigation. Inadequate? That instantaneous explosion of ecstasy had been 'inadequate'!

'Oh, my darling love . . .' Karim's voice caressed her with a husky tenderness as he drew her closer to him. 'Don't you understand how I feel? I don't know how much I hurt you. I don't know if you cried out. I don't even know if you begged me to stop. I felt only my own incredible pleasure!' His voice charged with turbulent anguish, he went on relentlessly, 'All men in Islam know that a man who wins the favour of a woman and then satisfies his own need before she has satisfied hers is inadequate.' The husky voice deepened until it was little more than a broken whisper. 'I love you. I've hurt you so much already. I could have spared you this.'

Vida had never known her heart could thunder with such breathtaking intensity. She must have misheard him! Savouring the intimate closeness of his body, breathing his scent and touching his skin, somehow she managed to seek the confirmation she craved for. 'You—you love me?'

She felt very young and very vulnerable before the glowing smouldering desire that transformed his face. 'Oh, yes, *mignonne*,' he breathed. 'I loved you from the first moment I set eyes on you ... and I've never stopped loving you!'

Dazed by the ardour of his protestations, bemused by their contradiction of everything that had passed between them since her enforced return, Vida shook her head in puzzlement. 'You tried very hard not to show it,' she protested, still unwilling to accept his avowal at face value. If it was just another cruel trick to hurt her ... She clamped her lower lip between her teeth to stop its quivering as she turned her reproachful eyes to study his expression. But there was tenderness, not cynicism, in his rueful explanation.

'I fought it like the devil himself. At first I thought I was still confusing desire with love, that after I'd possessed you, made you fulfil the cruel bargain you'd made with me, I'd see you as you truly were. But the more I tried to bend you to my will, the more abhorrent my plans became to me. Yesterday, when you ran away from me again, I had to face the truth— that desire was only one facet of my deep abiding love for the person I knew you to be. I knew then that what I had witnessed had been an act of desecration in which you were the victim ... and it was I who had betrayed you when I was too blind to realise it.'

She had despaired of ever hearing him say it! And now she was choked with happy tears, quite unable to speak. Karim's hands on her body spoke as eloquently as his tongue as he drew her closer to him, resting his cheek against her own. 'I knew I should go on my knees and beg for your forgiveness, but I was out of my mind with anxiety as time went by and there was no sign of you.' He gave a brief self-derisory laugh. 'By the time I got you back here I didn't know whether to slap you or kiss you or simply fall to the ground and thank God you were safe!'

How well she remembered the simmering fury of that encounter—and how it had resolved itself. 'You—you told me then that you loved me . . .' The words came as a shaky murmur as if she could still hardly credit their truth. 'But I didn't believe you . . .'

'And you repulsed me with such spirit I was convinced my blindness and stupidity had reaped their own reward!'

'I thought you were using the words as a ploy to persuade me to go to you so that afterwards you could reject and humiliate me,' Vida confessed sorrowfully.

'God knows, I deserve nothing but your hate!' She saw his mouth tauten with anguish and curled eager arms round his shoulders as he turned his head away from her in self-disgust.

'There were times when I thought I hated you,' she admitted honestly. 'When I realised how you'd deceived me by bringing me back here, and before then, when you never answered my letters.'

'I never read your letters.'

Vida stared blindly at his averted cheek as shock stiffened her spine. Surely both of them couldn't have gone astray? 'You never received them?' she gasped her amazement. No wonder her reception had been so abrasive! 'But, Karim...' she began unsteadily, breaking off as he moved and she saw the lines of strain that distorted his face.

'I received them all right,' he said tersely. 'But I was living in a kind of hell. My world as I'd known it had ceased to exist. Somehow I had to find the courage to fight back, and the last thing I could bear to read was your confession!' He paused, swallowing, while her dazed eyes stayed pinned to the facial evidence of his distress. When he continued his voice was hoarse with grief. 'You see, I'd already made my mind up. I threw your letters away—unopened...'

'Oh, no...' her protest was little more than a sigh as Karim continued his confession.

'Yet even then some deep unacknowledged remnant of my enduring love for you prevented me from destroying every trace of you. You'd written your name and address on the back of the envelopes and I copied it down before I tore them up, as if I knew that in the future I would send for you ... and you would come back to me.'

Vida swept her wide blue gaze over his dark face. 'So you never read my version of what happened? You only listened to what Haydon-Smith said to you, the lies he told.'

'To my eternal shame—yes,' Karim admitted thickly. 'I saw no reason then why he should lie. After all, you'd left me. I thought it was an admission of guilt.'

How could she blame him? Forgetting in that moment of tribulation that Karim had already expressed his faith in her, she cried out beseechingly,

'But he did lie! Oh, he did, Karim!' Agitation made her voice rise as she blinked back furious tears. 'But I can never prove it now. Tim's dead and . . .'

She had been going to say that even her own body had betrayed her by not providing the evidence of her virginity, but Karim cut across her agonised plea.

'But I can,' he told her harshly. 'Tonight I learned the full story about the degradation that was forced on you. I know the person and the purpose behind it.'

'Karim!' Astounded, she stared at the misery clouding his face. 'Who? Why? For God's sake tell me!'

For a moment he didn't answer and she could see the effects of his internal struggle mirrored in the depths of his eyes. Finally, with great effort, he said heavily, 'Fuad. My so-called-Uncle Fuad discovered that Haydon-Smith was a heroin addict desperate for funds and bribed him to dishonour you in my eyes so that our marriage would disintegrate. That it happened when it did was pure chance. Sooner or later you would have been alone and vulnerable and the result would have been the same.'

'But why?' Her voice husky with so many mixed emotions, Vida raised a hand to caress the lean cheek of the man she loved.

'Because, my darling, he was involved with a group of people who were trying to persuade me to return to Al-Khazar-ja to seek political power there. Not only did he believe it was your influence that had made me turn down the first representation made to me, but his plans had no room for my being married to anyone else than his own stepdaughter.' Karim watched her carefully, his face devoid of all expression. 'For months he'd been praising Laila's virtues as the ideal consort to a man of wealth and authority. He thought that with you discredited I would turn back to Islam and be happy to take her as my wife. As my father-in-law he envisaged a large share in the power he thought was mine for the taking.'

Wonderingly Vida shook her head. 'Karim ibn Ahmar,' she murmured, stunned that her life had been devastated by political intrigue. Then as she saw the reflected amazement on Karim's face, she added, 'Your mother told me something of the matter earlier this evening.'

Karim sighed softly, his arms enfolding her lovingly. 'Then perhaps you understand more fully than I'd hoped. As you say, Karim ibn Ahmar. A man who knew nothing about the real problems, a dupe, a puppet in the hands of people whose principles were unknown to him.' He shook his head. 'It was never a possibility. Even before I met you and lost my heart so completely. But if I'd realised the danger I was exposing you to . . .' He shuddered as she responded to him, burying her face in the warmth of his shoulder, trying to erase from her mind the moments of terror she had endured.

For a few seconds she lay silent, enjoying the touch of his naked body against her own, rejoicing in the sensation of his pulses beating in close harmony against her own, savouring the moment of intimacy as his hands swept in a loving caress down the smooth curves of her slender form.

It was the exoneration she had dreamed about for a year. But her greatest joy was in Karim's admission that he had re-found his faith in her without proof. Proof! She'd been so happy just to hear the facts, and she still didn't know how he had found out!

'How do you know?' she asked at last when she felt able to control the tremor in her voice.

'I'd already been searching in my mind for someone who had a motive to destroy our happiness,' Karim answered her quietly. 'It had to be someone close to us, who knew you were acquainted with Haydon-Smith. Someone who was at the Villa when the call from the police came through and who would have known I was leaving you alone. Allied to the pressure he had been putting on me, Fuad became a worthy suspect, and with that suspicion came a shocking realisation . . .'

There was something in the way he spoke, a terrible bitterness that sent a sudden chill weaving down Vida's spine. She couldn't comfort him, only relax against the pervading warmth of his golden skin as he went on relentlessly, 'I'd already been the architect of so much disaster in your life—and now I'd brought you back to my side. At a time when my injuries had healed and I'd regained my health and strength, when for the second time Fuad had breathed life into his own ambitions, I'd taken you back into my life and made you a potent threat to everything he still dreamed about.'

Sudden realisation illumined her. 'The businessmen who visited you the other night—Khalil said they were from Al-Khazar-ja . . .'

'They were,' he agreed grimly. 'They were honest patriots, but I gave them the same answer as before. I told them Karim ibn Ahmar had ceased to exist. When the army took over the country on the death of my grandfather and my uncle, his heir, fled to the United States, it was the end of a dynasty. The man they spoke to was Karim Gavigny, with a life and a destiny in which they had no share.'

He dipped his head to press a chaste kiss on Vida's forehead. 'I believe they accepted my decision as final this time. But it wasn't enough. If Fuad was the fanatic I thought him to be you could still be in danger. I knew last night that I must never tell you again that I loved you and needed you more than anything else in my life. I had to let you go for your own safety.'

'For ever?' she asked tremulously, unutterably relieved as he shook his head.

'Until the matter resolved itself.'

'And tonight it did?'

Yes.' The latent fury behind the word scorched her ears. 'Tonight Khalil came to me with Laila and begged me to listen to what she had to say—and my worst fears were confirmed.' His eyes flickered over her intent face. 'She had known for a long time that her stepfather wanted her to marry me. Since my recovery she had been a frequent visitor to the Villa in his company. He had hoped that proximity would endear us to each other,' he smiled grimly, 'Instead it was my brother who stole her heart . . . and she his.'

'He said he was in love . . .' Vida's eager interruption brought a twisted smile to Karim's lips.

'It was something Fuad hadn't foreseen,' Karim confirmed. 'He treated Laila as an unimportant member of his household, a tool to be used to further his own ambitions. Often he spoke without discretion in her hearing. It seems she had known of his implication in the break-up of our marriage, but she had been too scared to speak out or oppose him, until yesterday, when she heard him arranging for you to "disappear" while you were out by yourself in the Medina.'

'Karim!' Vida had gone cold with fear. Once or

twice she had fancied herself under surveillance, but she had dismissed the idea as ridiculous.

Karim's dark face was a hard mask as she lifted her gaze to watch the movement of the strong contours as he struggled for words. 'He'd come to the Villa before I got back from riding and seen your note. He intended to have you taken illegally from Morocco and returned to England in one final desperate attempt to make me change my mind.' Unresisting, Vida let him draw her head, down to rest against his heart. 'Fortunately he failed, *mignonne*, but the attempt was enough to make Laila decide where her loyalty lay. As soon as she could she came to Khalil, told him everything she knew and begged his protection.'

An icy hand clutched at Vida's heart. One look at Karim's face and she knew the matter hadn't ended there. Karim's absence from the party took on a sinister meaning. Fighting the shiver of fear that traversed her spine, 'You've been to see Fuad?' she whispered, her mouth dry with anticipation.

She felt Karim's hand fasten spasmodically on her arm. 'With murder in my heart and vengeance in my soul!' The dramatic words confirmed her worst fears. She gave a little moan, pressing her face into his shoulder, not attempting to stop the warm tears that dampened his skin. However justified he felt, Moroccan law would make him pay for any vengeance he had extorted, and she would lose him again . . .

He must have felt her sobs, for when he spoke again it was with resigned acceptance. 'Don't weep, *petite*. He'd gone. Laila had left a note telling him what she was going to do. He was never more than a crook and a brigand, but he was her kinsman and she felt she owed him that.'

'He's left Tangier?'

'Morocco too, I should imagine. There was no purpose in his staying. He knew he'd lost.' There was a deep sadness as Karim spoke again after a short silence. 'The Fahadazeen deserved a better ally than Fuad. Let us hope they'll find a leader amongst themselves. A man who understands the problems and pitfalls that await him. A man who will represent them with his heart as well as his name.'

Karim had made his decision, but Vida would have been stupid if she thought it had been without personal cost to his ideals.

She spoke quietly into the stretching silence as she visualised the dark fragile beauty of the Moslem girl.

'I owe Laila a great deal.'

'We both do,' Karim corrected gravely. 'She has my protection as well as my brother's. At first she'll live with my mother, then if she and Khalil are certain of their love for each other, I shan't stand in their way.'

His eyes regarded her with a deep smouldering passion, making her heartbeat race and her bones liquefy. 'When I came back from Fuad's deserted house I was determined to seek you out and tell you everything. I was going to beg you to stay here a little longer to give me the chance to show you how very much I loved you. But the Guedra had started . . .'

Vida suppressed the desire to interrupt him as she winced at the evidence of pain so hotly engraved in his dark eyes.

'And suddenly as I watched the dance, the Guedra girl was you, begging me to love you, to possess you.' He lifted her hand in an almost courtly gesture, pressing a kiss into its palm. 'I was terrified at the power of my own feelings, the strength of my need for you. I wanted you so much. Even if you had cared for me, I knew I lacked the self-control to love you with the gentleness and time you deserved. I had to get away . . .'

'There was another woman, then?' she asked gently.

'Not since the first day I saw you!' Karim denied hotly. 'I meant to take the Khamsin, open her up to maximum performance and drive until the raw speed brought its own satisfaction.'

'Or until you spun off the road and killed yourself!' Vida scolded roundly, before relaxing with a sigh against him. 'Dearest Karim . . . tonight I was that dancer. I came to you because I wanted you. I didn't need time or gentleness. I wanted you just as you came to me. Believe me . . . you didn't disappoint me!'

Some of the tenseness was fading from his face, but his eyes continued to search the flushed beauty of hers as if he could hardly believe her. At last he uttered a deep groan, moving his lips to seek the quivering flesh at the base of her throat, travelling slowly down to the pale orbs of her lovely breasts. 'I'll never cease to wish your initiation into the rites of love had been more leisurely, more tuned to your pleasure than mine.'

Stirring beneath the ardency of his touch, Vida sensed the traumatic power of his guilt. 'If it's your inadequacy that concerns you,' she teased softly, 'then surely there'll be other times to demonstrate your prowess?'

'Will there, Vida?'

In the dim light of the room there was a haunting sadness on his classic Arab features as he held her away from him and turned his liquid gaze on her sparkling blue eyes. 'The Guedra has a heady magic, my darling. It can be as intoxicating as vintage wine and far more dangerous, but its effects are ephemeral . . .' He expelled his breath in a deep shuddering sigh as pain twisted across his face, but his voice was controlled as he lifted one hand to brush a tendril of hair from her forehead with exquisite gentleness. 'When the sun rises its spell is replaced by reality. What are you telling me, *mignonne*? That you'll take pity on my loneliness and despair and stay another week, a fortnight, to the end of summer?'

Staring back into his expressive face, Vida saw for the first time the dampness on the long eyelashes as they clashed at each outer corner of his beautiful eyes. She knew what he was afraid of and hastened to put his mind at rest. However seductive the power of the Guedra with its explicit eroticism, it had been only a catalyst awakening her to herself.

'Reality is now, Karim,' she told him quietly, feeling a warm tingle of longing flow like molten lava through her veins as he continued to rake her face with his passionate devouring gaze. 'I'll stay as long as you want me to.'

'Then you'll never leave!' It was a triumphant cry of ownership.

Outside the incessant drumming of the Guedra continued, quickening to yet another climax. Soon they must rejoin their guests, but for a moment the world was theirs alone.

'Perhaps it would be for the best,' Vida said calmly, smiling up into the serious face of the man who, here in Morocco, was unquestionably still her husband.

In the past few days of trauma and distrust she was sure their earlier immature love had developed tenacious and enduring roots. It deserved the chance to blossom . . . and fruit.

An enigmatic smile tugged at the corners of her mouth as she allowed her hand to take its pleasure from stroking the trembling skin of his muscular chest, lowering her eyes in pretended humility. 'After all,' she told him, 'you already have my service and respect. I've tried my best to make myself beautiful for you like a good wife should, but that still leaves one important requirement . . . and that will take a little longer to fulfil.'

She glanced up at him from beneath the veil of long lashes that shielded her downcast eyes; saw, with utter joy, delight and pleasure replace the dark intensity that had drawn lines of pain round his sensuous mouth, as an answering glint enlivened the dark eyes that demanded she returned his unblinking stare.

Obediently she raised her head. Eyes as blue and unclouded as the North African summer sky could hide nothing, least of all the depth of her love for him.

'Bear me sons?' asked Karim, his voice breaking with barely held emotion.

There was only one answer she could make.

'*Mektoub*, Karim. *Mektoub*, my love.'

He reached for her, drawing her willing flesh against the heated surface of his own eager body, his hands vital messengers of the depth of his sincerity. 'But before my child is born I want the whole world to acknowledge you as my one and only wife—if it means we have to go through a dozen more marriage ceremonies! I want to bind you to me with every legal tie that exists,' he told her forcefully.

'There's no need . . .' Vida gasped the words through the mounting fever of need his questing mouth was arousing as it traversed the contours of her face with a gentle yet demanding fervour. 'I shall never want to leave you . . . but it if pleases you we can do whatever is necessary to comply with British law.'

'It pleases me, *mignonne*.' There was humour in his passion-thickened voice as he teased her, 'In fact I insist on it as your first act of wifely deference to my will.'

'Yes, Karim,' she said meekly, and then as he moved his hands with delicate purpose and infinite artistry, 'oh, yes, Karim . . . yes . . . yes!'

Outside in the darkness the guests sighed and stirred as the Guedra continued to weave its erotic magic, as fresh and compulsive now as it had been aeons ago in the love courts of the Tuareg warriors.

Inside the Villa, Karim and Vida came together in their own dance of love, bodies entwined, voices blending in mutual attestations of their passion.

The past was forgotten in the celebration of the present and the promise of the future as Karim proved his adequacy in all things.

**For the millions who can't read
Give the Gift of Literacy**

One out of five adults in North America
cannot read or write well enough
to fill out a job application
or understand the directions on a bottle of medicine.

**You can change all this by joining the fight
against illiteracy.**

For more information write to:
Contact, Box 81826, Lincoln, Neb. 68501
In the United States, call toll free: 800-228-3225

**The only degree you need
is a degree of caring**

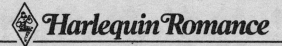
Harlequin Romance

Coming Next Month

Available in July wherever paperback books are sold, or
through Harlequin Reader Service.

In the U.S.
901 Fuhrmann Blvd.
P.O. Box 1397
Buffalo, N.Y. 14240-1397

In Canada
P.O. Box 603
Fort Erie, Ontario
L2A 5X3

Take 4 books
& a surprise gift
FREE

SPECIAL LIMITED-TIME OFFER

Mail to   **Harlequin Reader Service®**

In the U.S.   In Canada
901 Fuhrmann Blvd.   P.O. Box 609
P.O. Box 1394   Fort Erie, Ontario
Buffalo, N.Y. 14240-1394 L2A 5X3

YES!   Please send me 4 free Harlequin Presents® novels and my free surprise gift. Then send me 8 brand-new novels every month as they come off the presses. Bill me at the low price of $1.99 each*—an 11% saving off the retail price. There are no shipping, handling or other hidden costs. There is no minimum number of books I must purchase. I can always return a shipment and cancel at any time. Even if I never buy another book from Harlequin, the 4 free novels and the surprise gift are mine to keep forever.   108 BPP BP7F

*$2.24 in Canada plus 89¢ postage and handling per shipment.

Name	(PLEASE PRINT)
Address	Apt. No.
City	State/Prov. Zip/Postal Code

This offer is limited to one order per household and not valid to present subscribers. Price is subject to change.   DOP-SUB-1C

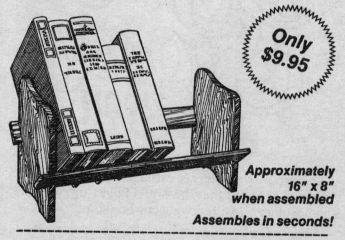